A Storm in Montana

Clancy Jarrett possesses a quick and violent temper and the citizens of Brannigan are careful not to cross him. But when his stagecoach hold-up is thwarted by three trail-herders his rage cannot be contained and with revenge on his mind soon there are bodies piling up. For the cowboys, their status as heroes is short-lived and when Jarrett learns they are escorting Kate Jeavons, a dance-hall girl whose sister he has captive, to testify against him, they are firmly in his sights.

Black clouds are forming overhead, but which storm will break first: the wild prairie rain, or the deadly guns of Jarrett and his crew?

A Storm in Montana

Will DuRey

A Black Horse Western

ROBERT HALE · LONDON

© Will DuRey 2013
First published in Great Britain 2013

ISBN 978-0-7198-0854-8

Robert Hale Limited
Clerkenwell House
Clerkenwell Green
London EC1R 0HT

www.halebooks.com

Typeset by
Derek Doyle & Associates, Shaw Heath
Printed and bound in Great Britain by
CPI Antony Rowe, Chippenham and Eastbourne

*For my friends, Pru, Deb and Helen, each a consistent source
of encouragement.*

PROLOGUE

It was dark when Jake Devane hitched the two horses in a stand of trees beyond the fence that surrounded Clancy Jarrett's yard. He approached the cabin stealthily, the derringer gripped tightly in his hand. Jake wasn't a gunman, the small, two-shot pistol being the only weapon he owned, but such was his confidence, his belief that he had the intelligence to outwit the men inside the shack, that no thought of failure entered his head. With luck, he wouldn't need the gun. If Alice was alone in a separate part of the cabin, he believed he could rescue her without alerting her captors; they would be long gone before she was missed, and after a brief stopover in Brannigan to collect Kate and the bag he'd left with her, long before dawn they would be on the road to Cheyenne, to a new life in another town, in another State.

His first furtive glance through the window boded well for a secret rescue. Alice wasn't in the room. Clancy was sitting at a table in the centre of the room, reading a newssheet and passing a comment about the editorial to Sepp Minto who sat opposite. Tulsa Jones, at the back of the room, was blowing softly into a harmonica, his big hands cupped around it so that it was almost completely hidden.

Jake half-rose from his crouched position, intending to make his way to the rear of the shack where he hoped to find Alice, but he paused at the realization that Ollie Dent, the fourth member of the gang, was missing. For a moment he pondered his next course of action and while he waited Alice came into the room. Despite the gloomy interior and the dirt-smudged window it was clear that she had suffered during the past days. Bruises discoloured her face, her hair was unkempt and she shuffled slightly as she walked, as though movement of her left leg caused her a great deal pain.

A rush of anger seared Jake's brain and it was heightened as a disparaging remark was directed at Alice by Clancy Jarrett. Sepp laughed and Tulsa quit blowing into the harmonica so that he could supplement Clancy's words with an insult of his own. Jake took a tighter grip on the derringer; even if it did hold only two shots he figured that a gun in the hand was better than three in their holsters.

But once again, as he prepared to move, stood upright to barge into the cabin and confront the men inside, his action was postponed. Tulsa had set aside his harmonica and was moving towards the door. For a moment Jake thought he'd been seen, but a wave of Tulsa's arm indicated that he was heading for the privy. Jake slipped around the side of the building as the door opened and watched from the shadows as Clancy's man sauntered past on his way to the wooden cubicle some twenty yards from the shack.

When he was inside and the door closed Jake crossed

the yard and waited close by until Tulsa emerged once more into the night. Pressing the small pistol into the stagecoach robber's back, Jake lifted the handgun from Tulsa's cut-away holster.

'Where's Ollie?' he whispered, his anger adding a rasping quality to his voice.

'In town. He'll be back soon.'

Jake wondered if the latter part of the answer was meant to make him believe he was in imminent danger. He pushed against Tulsa's back with this pistol, motioning him towards the cabin. As they got nearer he sensed Tulsa tense his muscles, knew he was going to attempt to turn the tables or yell out a warning. He let him get his hand on the door latch; then, as he began to push it open, he cracked him over the head with his own six-shooter. Tulsa fell into the cabin, hitting the floor with a loud crash. The commotion brought reaction from the other men in the room. Both jumped to their feet, their right hands dropping automatically to the weapons at their sides.

Jake shouted, thumbing back the hammer of Tulsa's gun to full cock so that Clancy and Sepp ceased in their efforts to arm themselves: 'Get your hands high.'

Reluctantly, the occupants obeyed. Clancy's expression signalled evil.

While Jake kept the men covered Alice took their guns and threw them outside. Then she found some rope and Jake trussed them tightly, talking as he did so, berating Clancy for his lack of trust.

'I suppose you heard I was moving on,' he said. 'Well, I couldn't stay with the mining company for ever. We've had a good run, Clancy, but they would have twigged before long that I was the source of your information. Sometimes the law acts slowly but usually they get there eventually. I always had plans to open my own casino, but I didn't intend running off with your money. You should have waited until I got back from Missoula; we'd have sorted this out amicably. When I came here tonight I still intended sharing, but now that I've seen what you've done to Alice you've lost any right to that money.'

'I have horses beyond the gate,' he told Alice; then to Clancy he added, 'We'll be long gone before you're free. No point trying to find us. Just accept that you and I are no longer partners.'

With his arms stretched behind him and then tied to the bindings around his ankles, it was awkward for Clancy to look up into Jake's face, but he did it despite the discomfort. 'You should kill me,' he said, 'cos I'll kill you when I catch you.'

The snarl in Clancy's voice unsettled Jake. For the first time that night a wedge of doubt lodged in his mind. He'd never killed a man before but at that moment, as he backed towards the door, he was overpowered with the thought that it was the right thing to do. The glare of hatred in Clancy's eye convinced Jake that his former partner would not let the matter end here. Without Clancy, he knew that Tulsa and Sepp wouldn't chase him, nor would Sheriff Oates. The people of Brannigan feared and hated Clancy. His death would be a cause for celebration, not revenge. Putting lead into Clancy was strong in his mind. Then, from outside, Alice called.

'Hurry Jake. Someone's coming.' With a sense of incompletion, Jake hurried Alice to where the horses were tethered.

The rider was approaching from the direction of

Brannigan, leaving little doubt as to his identity. Ollie Dent was the fourth member of the gang and Tulsa's warning that he would be back soon hadn't been a false prophecy. To avoid him, Jake and Alice rode up to the ridge behind the shack and headed east, away from town. As he spurred his mount on, panic gripped Jake. The realization that Clancy's release was imminent brought beads of sweat to his forehead. He regretted not pulling the trigger when he'd had the opportunity. Judging by the look that had been in Clancy's eyes he had no doubt that Jarrett would pursue him as soon as he got a saddle on a horse.

Jake's fears were well founded. Ollie Dent, having witnessed their dash for the high ground, soon cut free his partners from their bindings. Within minutes, with the exception of Tulsa Jones who remained groggy from the blow on the head, they were mounted up and giving chase.

Clancy and his men were more accustomed to being astride a horse and rapidly closed the distance between themselves and their quarry. Jake's increasing nervousness didn't help his and Alice's cause, nor did his indecisiveness. Heading east had not been his intention. He'd left his money in Brannigan and he was reluctant to stray too far from it. Perhaps if he had been thinking clearly he would have cared about it less, would have known that it could be retrieved by sending a telegram to Alice's sister from any town in any state in the Union, but he wasn't thinking clearly: fear had brought about confusion. Over and over Clancy's threat resounded in his mind until the only clear thought in his head was that he didn't know where he was going; he'd rescued Alice without any real

11

plan for making good their escape.

Twice they stopped, Jake yanking his horse to a halt in the hope that being motionless would also still the vortex of thoughts in his head, but the first stop was short-lived. Alice added to the confusion of thoughts by asking if Clancy's declaration was true: that Jake was the mastermind behind the local stagecoach robberies. Jake didn't answer, the sound of pursuit was too close behind. They kicked on with nothing resolved. The second pause lasted moments longer. The trail at this point was forty feet above the river, which flowed parallel to the road. It was Alice, seeing the strain of panic written on Jake's face, who urged them onwards. 'We must move on,' she cried. 'We've got to get as far away as we can.'

Jake nodded and they put spur to horse once more. However they progressed no more than half a dozen strides. Clancy, Ollie and Sepp emerged from the trees, barging their horses into those of Alice and Jake, evoking yells from the riders and startled neighs and snorts from the surprised horses, which reared and stumbled in the face of the sudden onslaught.

Jake's horse rose high on its hind legs as Clancy's mount struck against it; then Clancy discharged his pistol in front of its face. Jake clung to the reins and tried to grip more tightly with his knees, but when the fore hoofs slammed down on the solid rock road with juddering force, Jake lost control and fell from the saddle.

Alice was even less lucky. Her mount was first checked at the front by Ollie's horse; then, while unsettled and unbalanced, it was barged shoulder to shoulder by Sepp's. The impact was so great that even a better rider would have struggled to keep the horse upright. It slithered, its

A STORM IN MONTANA

forelegs crossed, then it toppled completely. Alice
screamed as she tried to adjust her position in the saddle
but at that narrow point of the trail her endeavour to stay
upright was hopeless. With terrified cries, horse and rider
slipped over the edge of the precipice. Amid the cruel
noise of tumbling dislodged rubble the hideous sounds of
the doomed horse arose to those on the trail as it slid into
the fast-flowing water below.

For a moment there was silence from those who
remained on the trail. Sepp Minto looked over the edge
but in the darkness of the night there was nothing to see.
He cupped a hand to an ear, exaggerating the fact that he
was listening to the rush of water.

'Gone,' he said. 'Water's moving so fast they'll be in the
Dakotas by morning.'

Ollie Dent laughed. Clancy, who hadn't taken his eyes
from the spread-eagled Jake Devane, leant forward in the
saddle. He waved the six-shooter he held. 'Perhaps you
should hand over that pop-gun you carry. Wouldn't want
you to get any ideas about pointing it at me again.'

Ollie Dent searched Jake and threw the pearl-handled
derringer to Clancy.

'No money in his pockets?' asked Clancy.

Ollie shook his head.

Jake thought of the money he had in Brannigan. Even
in this extreme moment when he knew his life hung in the
balance, he contrived a plan that he hoped would give
him the opportunity to get back to town.

'My money was in the saddle-bags on the horse that
went over,' he said, pointing to the precipice that led
down to the river.

'Too bad,' said Clancy, his finger tightening on his trigger.

'But there's another payroll due, Clancy. It'll be on Friday's stage.' Jake spoke quickly, unable to hide his fear, trying to grin as though they were still friends. 'Four days,' he added. In his mind's eye he envisaged himself making good his escape from Brannigan while these men held up the stagecoach somewhere south of town. They could have those takings, he thought: his war bag was full of everything he needed. Perhaps he'd forget about Cheyenne; Wyoming was too close to Clancy Jarrett for comfort.

'Four days,' repeated Clancy as though measuring how much living could be crammed into that time-scale.

'Usual shares,' said Jake, hoping his voice didn't betray his attempted deception.

Clancy laughed. 'I don't think so, Jake. Like I told you back at the cabin, you should have killed me when you had the chance.' His finger tightened against the trigger and the weapon spat out lead and flame. The bullet hit Jake between the eyes. Between them, Ollie and Sepp hurled the body over the precipice into the river below.

CHAPTER ONE

The chosen spot for the hold-up couldn't be faulted. Following the natural contours of the land, the trail was a series of twists down to the valley floor, and it was at the crown of the final bend, with the outcrops and boulders behind them, that the stagecoach driver removed his foot from the brake bar and began thinking of cracking the whip over the heads of the lead horses, or throwing small pebbles at their rumps to encourage them to pick up the pace for the final seven miles to Brannigan. This day, however both options were denied the driver.

The road agent's stone-coloured duster was buttoned high and hung low so that the only clothing visible to the two men riding high outside the coach were the wide-brimmed grey hat, the red-and-grey scarf that covered the lower half of his face and the dusty, unpolished foot of a brown right boot. He sat motionless on his dapple mare, straddling the trail, his head turned fully to the right to watch the approaching vehicle, the barrels of his shotgun pointed in the same direction. As the stagecoach hove into sight, he emptied one barrel into the air.

This wasn't the first coach that Denny Harvey had

driven to attract the attention of robbers. On previous occasions he had defied attempts to stop him and raced his horses for all they were worth. Today, too, such would have been his choice knowing that the closer they got to Brannigan the less likely any highwayman would be to continue the chase. But the matter was taken out of his hands.

First, the draught horses, surprised by the sudden noise in front, plunged and reared, each trying to change direction and each dragging the others off balance. Denny could see one of the middle pair slither, its fore legs buckle as though it might sink to its knees. If it went down, if *any* of them went down, it would be a catastrophe for the coach and its passengers. Unsettled and nervous, the horses' neighing and whinnying added to their own confusion. Wary that thrashing limbs would become entangled with the leathers and chains of harness, Denny hauled on the reins in an effort to regain control of his team.

His second reason for not encouraging the horses into headlong flight was due to his partner, Bullwhip Saxon, a man with a querulous spirit and an inborn reluctance to comply with the wishes of strangers. Like Denny, when a highwayman wanted to stop a stagecoach his instinct was to make the horses run faster, but this time it was different. The spooked team had the coach lurching and swaying in such fashion that he wasn't able to bring his rifle to bear on the rider ahead, and the angle at which that road agent's gun and those of his companions who were now emerging from the roadside trees made it clear that any attempt to escape would result in someone's death.

'Haul 'em in, Denny,' Bullwhip shouted. 'Haul 'em in.'

One of the riders grabbed the bridle of a lead horse to bring the coach to an awkward halt. Swiftly he unhitched the six horses from the vehicle's shafts then, with shouts and shots on the air, provoked the animals into headlong flight along the trail towards Brannigan.

Another of the robbers ordered Denny and Bullwhip to throw away their weapons then demanded the strongbox. It crossed Bullwhip's mind to bluff it out, tell the robbers they weren't carrying one this trip, but the masked man made it clear that he knew exactly what they had in the box.

'You're carrying the mineworker's wages,' he shouted. 'The box is either under your feet or tied into the luggage hold behind.'

Lacking any alternative, Denny threw down the box.

Using an iron lever, the outlaw prised open the padlock and transferred the bundles of paper money into a canvas bag.

Meanwhile, the fourth member of the gang ordered the passengers out of the vehicle. They numbered four, three men and a lady. The married couple were the first to surrender what little wealth they carried with them: a slim wallet from him and some simple jewellery from her. Next was a fat man for whom the heat of the day seemed to be a greater enemy than the man with the gun. Incessantly, he dabbed at his face with a cotton square to soak up the beads of sweat that developed. He had a fatter wallet and a gold pocket-watch to donate. The last passenger was a slim young cleric, willing enough to contribute his mean pocket money to the collection but grimly determined to hang on to the envelope containing $500 destined for the church at Brannigan. When the struggle for the money became more than a matter of words, Bullwhip yelled in protest at the gunman's violence. His shout was answered by a shot from the gunman's revolver, the zing of the bullet passing his ear was warning enough to interfere no further.

Beyond the southern ridge that led to the open-range country of Montana, three cowboys had pulled rein. Al Dunnin, the eldest of the trio, spoke first.

'Sounded like a shotgun,' he declared. 'The road to Brannigan is just beyond that rise.'

'Should we take a look?' young Walt Dickers asked, his voice betraying more than a hint of excitement.

'A hunter.' Bart Sween spoke slowly, attempting to dampen the lad's eagerness. 'Chasing rabbit, I suppose.' The look he exchanged with Al, however, showed a lack of faith in his own explanation. There was rarely an innocent explanation for gunfire, and both he and Al had seen the far-off stagecoach descending the hill trail only a short while ago. He gave the lead rein of his pack horse to Walt and motioned for Al to do likewise. 'Wait here with the animals,' he told the youngster. 'We'll take a look.'

No sooner had Bart and Al put spur to horse than two more shots sounded from beyond the rise. Unwilling to miss out on any action, Walt dismounted, ground hitched the two pack animals left in his charge, then leapt back into the saddle and chased after his friends. A fourth gunshot reached their ears as they breasted the ridge and looked down on the action around the besieged stage-coach. 'Come on,' Bart said to Al and, drawing his revolver, plunged over the edge, taking the shortest route to the aid of the stricken passengers.

It was the outlaw on the dapple mare who first saw the

approaching riders. 'Hurry,' he yelled at the man who was gathering in the booty from the passengers. 'We've got company.' He fired the second barrel of the shotgun as the newcomers reached the trail some 200 yards behind the stranded coach. The spread of shot over such a distance minimized its effectiveness but the blast spurred his partners to reach for their guns while simultaneously making for their horses.

The passengers inside the coach crouched low, reducing the risk of being hit if a gun battle developed. Bullwhip and Denny Harvey, unarmed and therefore unable to contribute to the plight of the robbers, sat atop the coach watching the approach of their would-be rescuers, remaining alert for any opportunity to assist.

'Come on,' the mounted outlaw yelled, urging the others to catch their horses and put distance between themselves and the oncoming cowboys, 'we've got what we wanted.' He had drawn his six-gun, but clutching the shotgun and the reins detracted from the accuracy of his shooting. With the money in the bag he saw no reason to tarry by the stagecoach and risk injury or capture.

Other than a couple of misdirected shots back along the trail, the outlaws were unable to muster a coordinated response to the unexpected attack. Their efforts were concentrated on catching and climbing on to their horses. The last man to do so was the one carrying a linen bag, which now contained the contents of the strongbox and those items taken from the passengers. The remainder of the gang was now in full flight and by the time he mounted he was twenty yards behind.

Once they'd gained the more level surface of the trail Al and Bart had begun to return the gunfire and, unhindered, their shooting was more accurate than that of the robbers. Even so, although he would never admit it, Al's shot which hit the last outlaw was nothing more than luck. He was still fifty feet from the coach when he fired and he was well aware that the accuracy of any pistol over such a distance could not be guaranteed. But hit the fleeing outlaw he did, extracting from the man a pain-filled yell as he slumped forward on to his horse's neck.

The impact of the bullet had shattered the outlaw's shoulder blade; the resulting pain was so intense that only thoughts of self-preservation filled his mind. Although barely conscious, he hung on to his horse and followed the other members of the gang away from the scene of the hold-up; that he had dropped the linen bag he neither noticed nor cared about until there were many miles between himself and the stranded stagecoach.

When they reached the stagecoach, with the robbers in full retreat, Bart and Al reined in to enquire if anyone was hurt and were relieved to learn that, apart from the blow the churchman had taken, everyone was fine. Walt Dickers, still a few strides behind his friends and having adopted a different line of approach in an effort to catch up, didn't stop. He had seen something that had escaped the notice of his friends. Walt had seen the wounded man drop the bag and was now going to retrieve it. When he returned to the coach with all the valuables intact he was hailed a hero by all the passengers. Walt was happy to bask in their praise and his older friends were content to let him do so.

Satisfied that the passengers were safe and that the outlaws had fled, Al Dunnin rode off in search of the scattered horses. Bullwhip saw to it that each passenger got back the money and valuables that had been taken from them and gave voice to his belief that the stageline or the mine-owners should reward the three cowboys who had come to their aid. Among the rescued passengers this was a popular suggestion and the fat man, Silas Wainwright, professing a degree of political influence, assured Bart and Walt that he would write letters to both Jeb Friar, the owner of the stageline, and the Minnesota Mining Company proposing that such courage should be marked by some financial reward. The churchman, Reverend Smallwood, echoed Silas Wainwright's declaration, stating once again the importance of the money he was carrying for the church at Brannigan.

Young Walt Dickers swelled with pride as he listened to the many compliments that the travellers directed his way, and the promise of a reward brought a grin to his face that stretched from ear to ear. Bart Sween, on the other hand, put no trust in such blandishments. They would get to Brannigan, fill the order for supplies that old man Jefford, the ranch owner, had given him and, in the morning, at first light, they would be on the way back to the herd no richer than they were now. But he kept his own counsel, no need yet to end his young friend's joy.

Dragging traces had so confused the startled team that they'd run less than two miles before the sight and smell of the river had brought them to a standstill in the cold water. Within twenty minutes Al had caught them and jogged them back up the trail. While they were being reharnessed to the coach, Walt rode back across the ridge to where he'd ground hitched the pack animals; when he returned everyone was ready to continue the journey. Al, Bart and Walt rode alongside the coach for the remainder of the journey to Brannigan.

*

Clancy Jarrett rode the dapple mare hard, avoiding any recognized trail, weaving among the high pines on the wooded slope to the river. With his men strung out behind, he crossed the narrow stream and gained the height above the far bank before halting in the cover of the tree line. While he waited for the other three to join him he kept a watchful eye on the river crossing and, beyond that, their back trail. Satisfied that they were not being pursued he took a moment to pull down the scarf that had covered his face, then he removed the long coat, which he rolled up and tied behind his saddle.

'Nobody following,' declared Tulsa Jones, who was the first man to rein in beside Clancy. 'I don't think they chased us very far.'

'Do you think they were lawmen, Clancy?' Sepp Minto pulled away the neckerchief from his face and wiped it across his brow before retying it around his neck.

Clancy snorted with contempt. 'If they were lawmen they would still be chasing.' Sepp wasn't sure whether Clancy's sneer was intended to signify his amusement at Sepp's lack of ability to come to such a conclusion, or only his own scant regard for the possibility of being captured by a lawman.

'Hey!' exclaimed Tulsa. 'Here comes Ollie. Looks like he's been hit.'

The three watched the slow progress of the fourth gang member as his pony, following the scent and sounds of the other horses, wended its way among the trees to where they waited. Ollie Dent was slouched in his saddle, his face bore a paleness that not even the three-day absence of a razor could disguise. Tulsa rode forward to grasp the bridle of Ollie's horse and bring it alongside the other two.

It took only a quick inspection of the wound for Tulsa to form an opinion. 'It's bad.'

'Let's get him back to the shack,' Clancy said. 'We'll do what we can for him.'

'He needs a doctor.'

'You want to take him into Brannigan? You think Sheriff Oates won't be on the lookout for someone with such a wound? No, Ollie will have to take his chance that we can get the bullet out.'

Tulsa and Sepp Minto exchanged troubled looks. They'd ridden with Ollie a long time. Any one of them could have stopped a bullet. You didn't desert your partners in time of need any more than you expected them to desert you. Besides, treating such a wound was beyond their ability. It wasn't as if the bullet had hit some fleshy part of the leg, or an arm, this one had done serious damage and already Ollie had lost a lot of blood.

'There are doctors in other towns,' Tulsa said. 'We'll take him to Blackwater. Or bring their doctor out to the shack.'

'We'll do nothing until we've shared the money,' said Clancy, but it was clear he would oppose anything that brought them to the attention of the law. He rode around the horse upon which Ollie, his face etched with agony, slumped. 'Where is it?' demanded Clancy, accusation in the sound of his voice and the gleam in his eye. 'Where's the money?'

Sepp Minto climbed down from his horse and began to search Ollie and the saddle-bags. 'It's not here. He must have dropped it.'

Clancy Jarrett's temper was always on a short fuse but since Jake Devane's betrayal, being around him had been like living close to a simmering volcano, a cataclysmic eruption imminent and likely to destroy anything within range. He grabbed the collar of Ollie's shirt and pulled him upright. 'Where's the money?'

The torment of pain extracted a moan from Ollie that seemed to emanate from the centre of his being. When Clancy again asked where the money had been dropped it was Sepp, sympathetic to his friend's condition, who spoke. 'Why don't we ride back. We'll find the bag along the trail.'

'Don't be a fool,' stormed Clancy. 'He dropped it back at the stagecoach. They've got it all back. They'll be laughing at our pathetic hold-up.'

'He was shot, Clancy,' said Tulsa. 'He couldn't help it.'

Clancy turned an angry face to Tulsa. 'Shot! Yes. But not well enough.' Instantly he drew his gun and fired two bullets into Ollie's chest. The dead man fell to the ground.

Sepp had smirked a couple of nights earlier when Clancy had killed Jake Devane with the same cruel coldness, but he didn't laugh this time. Tulsa almost spoke, almost said there had been no need to kill Ollie, but Clancy still had his gun in his hand and the expression on his face was the coldness of a killer who was ready to strike again. So when Clancy ordered them to hide Ollie's body, they dragged it among some trees in silence – acutely aware that in this isolated spot it was unlikely ever to be found.

CHAPTER TWO

News of the hold-up and rescue spread quickly through the town when the travellers eventually arrived. From the top of the coach, Bullwhip told the whole story to those gathered outside the depot, curious as to its late arrival.

'These men deserve a reward,' he finished, directing the last remark at Fred Walker, the man in charge at the depot.

'It'll all go in my report,' said Fred, his facial expression as bland as his words, making it clear that such decisions were beyond his authority. 'Here comes Sheriff Oates. Tell your story to him.'

The lawman bustled along the street. Were it not that he walked as though he was still astride a horse he would have been an imposing figure. The fact that his legs were never fully straight deprived him of four or five inches of his true height. Nonetheless, his torso was long and broad. His face was big and dominated by a moustache which drooped to his chin at either side of his mouth. He was rubbing a hand across his lips as he approached, as though news of the coach's arrival had interrupted a meal.

'What happened,' he asked.

Although the question had been directed at Fred Walker, it was Bullwhip who replied, reciting his first account almost word for word, almost like a mantra, even repeating the same conclusion: that Al, Bart and Walt deserved a reward.

'Did you recognize anyone?' Sheriff Oates asked, ignoring completely the subject of reward.

Bart Sween had asked the same question on the ride into Brannigan and in reply the stagecoach guard had revealed that there had been a number of attacks during the past months. The chief suspect was a man called Clancy Jarrett, a violent man who made his own rules and expected everyone else to obey them. He and his crew lived in a shack on a patch of land west of town. It wasn't a working ranch, for there was no other livestock and no crops were grown. When he and his men came to Brannigan they often terrorized the townspeople but always had witnesses to vouch for the fact that their behaviour was within the law, witnesses who were coerced into speaking on Clancy Jarrett's behalf. That Sheriff Oates tolerated Jarrett's visits to town didn't sit well with Bullwhip.

'Like I said,' Bullwhip replied, 'they had their faces covered. If I was able to tell you who did it I would.' He spat on the ground, a sign of his anger and frustration. 'But one of them stopped a bullet. If the doc gets called out to the Jarrett place you might have your answer.'

There were murmurs from the crowd, which were all ignored by the sheriff. 'You all need to come down to my office,' he said, his look sweeping over those on top of the coach, the passengers who had stepped out and the three cowboys who were still astride their horses. 'I need all of you to tell me what happened so that I can make out a report.'

'Pointing a pencil at Jarrett won't get him to surrender,' grumbled Bullwhip.

'You got some reason to suppose it was Clancy Jarrett?' asked Sheriff Oates.

'You know who is behind these robberies as well as I do, Sheriff.'

'Bring me proof and I'll arrest him.' Sheriff Oates scanned the faces of those gathered. 'That goes for every-one. I can't do anything without proof and up to now nobody has brought any.' There was a hint of accusation in his words: that if the citizens thought he was failing them then they needed to examine their own behaviour first. 'So,' he continued, 'I need those concerned to come to my office so that I can record the details of this incident.'

'I wonder,' interrupted a man who had hurried across the street shortly after the arrival of the stagecoach in town, 'if I can speak to one of the gentlemen who per-formed the rescue. I'm sure you don't need all of them to make a statement, Sheriff?'

'Perhaps not,' said Sheriff Oates, 'but it doesn't neces-sarily mean that any of them will want to speak to you.' The three cowboys turned quizzical eyes to the man in the street. He was in shirtsleeves, a sign that their arrival had brought about a sudden interruption to his normal working day. 'Mr Patrick,' the sheriff explained, 'runs the newspaper office. If one of you wants to talk to him I have no objection.'

Walt Dickers beamed. 'I'll get my name in the newspa-per?'

'You certainly will,' said the sandy-haired newspaper proprietor, 'you and your associates.'

Walt turned his attention to Al and Bart, seeking their approval.

'You speak to Mr Patrick, Walt. Al and I will go with the sheriff. When we're through there we'll head along to the merchants for the supplies, then we'll meet up at the Prairie Rose.' Bart pointed to a saloon further along the street.

'You can have a beer,' Al told him. 'Nothing stronger.'

Even Al's words, delivered in his usual terse manner, like some kind of a rebuke, couldn't chase the grin from Walt's face. He dismounted, hitched his pony to a rail and followed Mr Patrick across the street into the wood-framed building which bore the name *The Clarion* over the door.

Walt gave the facts of the incident and Saul Patrick embellished them into a drama designed to grab the attention of his readers. It also confused and embarrassed Walt with its implication that he, and he alone, had engaged four highwaymen in a gun battle and given chase until he'd wrested the stolen goods from them. The articulate newspaperman swept aside the young cowboy's protestations, persuading him that the act of recapturing the money made him the central figure in the drama. When Walt left the newspaper office with the assurance that the next issue would be on the street before he left town, he was as happy and proud as he had ever been in his life.

Silas Wainwright was a man who needed to be the centre of attention. Nothing gave him greater pleasure than that his voice should dominate whichever room he occupied. Consequently, he hadn't stopped talking since he'd first taken up a position at the end of the long bar in the

Prairie Rose, regaling those present with his own account of the foiled stagecoach robbery. But now the customers were growing weary of the story, and of his voice.

An attack on the stagecoach was no longer a rare event and most citizens, while muttering expressions of agreement to Wainwright's call for the robbers to be apprehended, had no intention of doing anything about it. Like Bullwhip, they had their suspicions about the identity of the robber but, unlike the stagecoach guard, the name of Clancy Jarrett would never cross their lips. Most of them had witnessed demonstrations of Jarrett's violence in the past and none of them was anxious to become the target of his next outburst.

So, not only were they tired of Wainwright's voice but they were also wary lest Clancy Jarrett should come into the saloon whilst the robbery was the main topic of conversation. All they wanted now was to get back to games of chance, whiskey and saloon girls.

When Walt Dickers pushed his way through the batwing doors his presence gave second wind to the fat man's oratory.

'My young friend,' he called, stepping forward to welcome Walt and usher him to the bar, 'let me be the first to buy you a drink, scant reward for your earlier heroic behaviour but given with humble gratitude. Gentlemen,' he continued, raising his voice in a fresh address to the whole room, 'here is one of the gallant trio who fought off the roadside villains.' He wrapped an arm around Walt's shoulder as they stood at the bar, presenting him to the room for their commendation.

Walt had been hoping that his friends, Al and Bart, had finished their business at the mercantile store and were waiting for him inside the Prairie Rose. He'd never been in a saloon before, leastways, not alone and not to drink alcohol. He wasn't sure that he was acting within the law by doing so now. Different towns applied different restrictions regarding those who could and could not purchase alcohol, but Walt figured he'd lie if anyone asked his age. His awkwardness showed in his expression, but most of the men in the room put that down to unease caused by the effusive welcome from Silas Wainwright: it was unnatural behaviour for men living west of the Missouri. But they didn't hold Walt responsible for that and, when he began to relax and allow his earlier good humour to show on his face, he was quickly accepted by the men in the room.

Because of his youth and apparent naïvety he was soon the centre of attention and the good-natured manner in which they sported with him was similar to what he'd enjoyed on recent nights around the campfire with the other tired drovers. His new acquaintances quickly persuaded him to give his version of the hold-up and sitting at a table with a glass of beer in one hand he tried to recall the story as Saul Patrick, the newspaper man, had written it. Suddenly a girl was sitting on his knees. She was one of the saloon girls in a black, satin dress with a large red feather in her hair. There was laughter all around the room as the youth, unable to conceal his embarrassment, was transfixed by the expanse of bare bosom before him.

'His face is redder than your hair, Kate,' someone shouted, causing another wave of laughter.

But the merriment came to an abrupt halt when the batwings crashed against the wall. Clancy Jarrett glowered at the scene before him. Tulsa Jones and Sepp Minto stood at either side, a step behind. For a moment there was total silence in the room. No one was certain how much of Walt's braggadocio the new arrivals had overheard, and certainly no one was prepared for what happened next. The townsfolk's dislike of Clancy Jarrett was based on his practice of goading peaceful men into fights. Some of them, with the assistance of his crew, he beat mercilessly, while the less lucky were gunned down merely to entertain himself when he knew he was faster with a gun.

This day, however, the violence erupted in a moment and was over before anyone could register a protest. Clancy rushed forward, grabbed Kate and pulled her to her feet. The bodice of her dress tore in his hands as he thrust her across the room. 'That's my girl you're mauling,' he spat at Walt.

'I wasn't—' Walt began, his hand lifting from the table in a defensive gesture.

'Don't go for that gun,' yelled Clancy, while at the same time he drew his own and fired two shots into Walt's chest. The lad fell to the floor, his shirt afire from the closeness of the gunfire and his boot heels drumming a momentary death tattoo.

'You all saw that,' Clancy announced to the room. 'Self-defence. He went for his gun first.'

Momentarily, Tulsa Jones and Sepp Minto were as stunned by the sudden killing as everyone else in the room. It hadn't escaped their notice that the recent killings of Jake Devane and Ollie Dent had marked a new ruthlessness in their leader, that ever since Jake Devane had made it known he was moving to Cheyenne Clancy's temper had become more volatile. But no one had been around to witness the killings of Jake and Ollie: this one had been undertaken in the full light of day in the centre of Brannigan. Still, they found their voices and supported Clancy's claim of self defence. It was unlikely that anyone would disagree, for most of those nearest the door had already quit the saloon to avoid giving testimony when the sheriff arrived.

CHAPTER THREE

An accident at a river crossing had brought Bart Sween and his friends to Brannigan. A wheel of the chuck wagon had dropped into an underwater crevice and its awkward position had caused it to crack as the driver urged the horses to pull it free. The wagon had slumped at the back corner and water had flowed over the high boards. Although they were able to repair the wheel, the provisions that had been spoilt by river water needed to be replaced.

Virgil Jefford's knowledge of the territory was good enough to know that if a horseman set out at dawn he could reach Brannigan before the end of day and would be able to rejoin the cattle drive before the following sunset. So he'd made a note of the cook's requirements and dispatched Bart and Al Dunnin with packhorses to buy the replacement goods. In a moment of compassion he'd allowed young Walt Dickers to go with them. He liked the young novice and felt a certain responsibility for him.

For most of the drive Walt had ridden drag, his eyes and throat permanently full of dust. Nobody, the trail boss assumed, would resent the lad's absence for two days; more likely they would tease him all the more about how much whiskey he'd drunk and how many girls he'd chased while away from the herd. Virgil was confident that with Al and Bart as his companions, Walt was unlikely to get into any trouble.

The initial excitement caused by their arrival with the stagecoach had now died down; their statements had been given to Sheriff Oates, and young Walt was ensconced with the newspaper proprietor across the street. Bart and Al now set about their own tasks. Al took the horses to the livery at the far end of town, paid for feed and stabling and got caught up in a conversation with the horse-keeper who wanted a private recounting of the interrupted hold-up.

The gunshots reached their ears as Al was bringing his story to a close. The liveryman, who, while Al was talking, had kept his own counsel about the probable identity of the robbers, spat on the ground. 'Sounds like Clancy Jarrett's in town,' he said.

Al recognized the name from the earlier chatter of the stagecoach driver and cast a look up the street. Most of the activity appeared to be outside the saloon, where he'd agreed to meet up with Bart and Walt. Men were gathered on the boardwalk, peering through the windows and clustered around the swing doors. He figured he'd find out the cause of the shooting when they were together. With a farewell flick at the brim of his hat, Al left the stableman and crossed the street to the mercantile store.

The storekeeper tried to make light of the gunfire, telling Bart that Brannigan was a quiet community. His sly look up the street, however, betrayed his concern. When

34

Bart saw Al approaching he took his leave of the mercantile store, insisting that he and his friends would return early next morning to collect the goods he'd purchased.

The Butte Hotel had been the next stop on their list, to fix up beds for the night, but when Al mentioned the stableman's notion that the shooting might be attributable to Clancy Jarrett they chose instead to make their way to the Prairie Rose. Although it was a slim chance, they figured they might be able to identify him as one of the robbers.

Across the West it was rare for saloons like the Prairie Rose not to resound to the raucous voices of drinking men and the tinny music of an upright piano, but even before Al and Bart pushed their way through the batwing doors they were conscious that there existed only a muted echo of what was expected. When they stepped inside, even that murmur died away almost completely. Momentarily, the heads of those who had remained in the saloon turned in their direction, but then, one by one, as the two cowboys tried to read the expressions on those faces, their gazes dropped to their glasses and the cards that lay scattered on the tables around which they sat.

The only man giving wind to words was Sheriff Oates. His voice sounded gruff, angry and sad as he supervised the efforts of four men. 'Take him to Seth Simm's parlour,' he told them. He turned as he spoke, curious as to the identity of the newcomers to the saloon. Until then, he had obscured the object of the men's labour from Al and Bart, but now they could see that a corpse had been lifted on to a flat board and that the men had positioned themselves at the corners, ready to obey the sheriff's command.

Sheriff Oates looked at the two cowboys, then at the body on the board. He shuffled his feet and hunched his shoulders, the manner of his movements expressing both embarrassment and apology. 'He got into a fight,' he explained.

Bart regarded the body on the board. The eyes were wide open and the mouth agape. Death had come as an unwelcome surprise to Walt Dickers. 'Who did this?' he asked, his hands moving swiftly to lower the boy's eyelids and push up his loose jaw.

'The boy went for his gun first,' Sheriff Oates told him, ignoring the question he'd been asked.

'That's a lie,' replied Bart. 'That boy never fired a gun to hustle along a lazy steer.'

'There are witnesses,' the lawman said, but there wasn't a lot of conviction behind his words.

'Did you put his pistol in his holster, Sheriff?'

'No.'

'It never got pulled, did it?' Bart's mouth was a grim line, his anger demonstrated by his stance and the set of his body.

'He assaulted a woman,' the sheriff offered as justification.

'Did you see this yourself, Sheriff?' Al Dunnin asked.

'Well, no.'

'Have you questioned the man who did this?'

'I've told you, there were witnesses. Your friend was drinking, messing with one of the girls. Her man caught him at it and when confronted he went for his gun. He was warned not to do it. It was self-defence. Kill or be killed. That's the way it was told to me and nobody's offered a different version.'

'This girl, she works here?' Bart asked.

No one answered at first. Sheriff Oates stretched his

arms before him, patting air, attempting to pacify the cowboy. 'Her story won't be any different.'

'You haven't spoken to her?'

'She's hurt. I'll question her tomorrow.'

'It needs to be done now, Sheriff. Who is she? Where is she?'

It was the barman who answered. He was standing by with a bucket and mop to wash away Walt's blood, and he had a box of sawdust to spread over the floor. 'It was Kate,' he said. 'She's upstairs.' His eyes lifted to the balcony at the far end of the room.

Sheriff Oates protested as Bart and Al headed for the stairs. 'I forbid it,' he said.

'You're not prepared to ask her what happened, Sheriff, so we will,' Bart told him. 'We mean her no harm. We just want to hear the story from her own lips.' Bart and Al almost ran up the stairs. Sheriff Oates, conscious that his authority in the town was being tested, decided that his best course of action was to be present when the cowboys spoke to Kate. In his ungainly fashion, he hurried after.

Guided by signals from the barman below, Bart knocked at the appropriate door and went in without awaiting an answer. Two girls were sitting on the edge of the bed. It wasn't difficult to decide which one was Kate because there was dried blood from a cut on her upper lip and a lump the size of a quail's egg at the side of her left eye. A patch of skin on her left cheek was bruised purple. She looked up, startled by the intrusion, cowering slightly against her companion as though she expected Al and Bart to be the bringers of more violence. The other girl, older but wearing a low-necked dance-hall dress similar to Kate's, found her voice first, ordering the men from the room.

'Can't do that,' said Al. 'We need to hear what happened downstairs. That boy who was killed was our friend.'

'What have you been told?' Kate asked.

'What we've been told would imply that Walt did that to you,' Bart said, pointing at her face. 'I just don't believe it.'

The girl said nothing for a moment, glaring defiance at them, it seemed, but in fact she was too numb with pain and fear to respond. Eventually she dropped her gaze and spoke. 'Then you should believe it. Just accept that it happened and go. Leave Brannigan. You can't do anything for your friend now.'

'We can clear him of being a woman beater,' said Al, 'and bring his killer to justice.'

Kate laughed. It wasn't a pleasant sound. Its bitterness flooded over into her words. 'You won't get anyone to testify against Clancy in this town.'

The name struck Bart like a hammer. 'Clancy! Clancy Jarrett?'

The girl didn't know how or why the name of Clancy Jarrett was known to these strangers but it was clear that whatever they knew of him left no room for doubt that the killing had not been as the result of a fair fight. The hard glint of determination that shone in Bart's eyes and the expression on the face of the other one, as she glanced quickly at Al, spoke clearly of their loyalty for the dead boy and that their duty as his friends was clear. It was the code of the West; a man killed in a fair fight was buried by his friends, but for an unpunished murder they often sought revenge. Such seemed to be the message written on the two faces before her.

For a moment she experienced a sensation of hope, but it soon disappeared. At the moment, these men were angry at the death of their companion and thought only of confronting his killer, but if Clancy Jarrett ever got to hear that these men were seeking revenge for the death of their friend he would never meet them face to face. He would ambush them, or shoot them in the back and concoct some story that his friends would corroborate. He had this town so terrified that no one would ever testify against him.

Bart had turned his attention to Sheriff Oates, who had followed Al into the room. 'Clancy Jarrett, Sheriff. Who is running this town, him or you?'

'Now hold it a minute,' began Sheriff Oates, 'I've got no reason to arrest Clancy Jarrett for anything.'

'I haven't been in this town half a day but I've heard the rumours that he's behind the stagecoach robberies. Have you spoken to him about those?'

'I'm not responsible for the law beyond the town limits,' he declared in his gruff manner. 'Besides, no one has ever brought proof of his involvement. The law doesn't act on rumour.'

'The law doesn't seem to act on murder either. How many people has he killed here in Brannigan?'

'None that haven't been witnessed as fair fights.'

'Well, the killing of Walt Dickers wasn't a fair fight and if you aren't prepared to arrest him for it then I reckon it is up to me and Al to settle it.'

'Listen to me, Sween.' The sheriff straightened his back, looked Bart in the eye, prepared to demonstrate his authority as the lawman of Brannigan, 'I'll have no revenge killings in this town. If you start trouble I'll throw you in jail. You've done the town a service so let me give you some advice. Saddle up and get back to your herd.'

'Can't do that, Sheriff. Our horses are tired and the provisions we've paid for won't be ready for collection until the morning. We won't be leaving before then. Now, perhaps you can tell me where I'll find Clancy Jarrett.'

Sheriff Oates didn't tell them where to find Clancy, he only repeated that he would hold Bart and Al responsible if there was further violence in Brannigan. Then he pushed Al aside as he stormed out the room. Bart followed, but before he reached the door, Kate spoke to him.

'Mister,' she said, her voice low, heavy with concern, 'do yourself a favour. Believe that the boy did this to me and that he went for his gun first. Then do what the sheriff suggested. Get on your horses and ride away from here.'

Bart paused before answering, convinced himself that the watery plea in her eyes was genuine, that she wanted him to leave town because she didn't believe he could win any fight with Clancy Jarrett.

'No,' he said, 'I can't do that.' He touched his hat, stepped outside the room and closed the door.

By nightfall, Al and Bart had still not crossed Clancy Jarrett's path, by which time, although they were no less determined in their quest, the fire of their anger had subsided. Sheriff Oates had waited for them outside the Prairie Rose and issued another warning that he would hold them responsible for any further violence in the town, but this was tempered by a proffered olive branch, a proposal that the town would pay the burial expenses because of Walt's part in preventing the stagecoach robbery.

Bart's anger had been at full tide at that moment and he had angrily dismissed the offer, telling the sheriff that his town wasn't a fit place for good men to lie. They would take him back to Virgil Jefford, bury him someplace on the open range, above the trail where the herds were driven to the railhead.

So they went to the funeral parlour to arrange to collect Walt's body when they left town. Seeing the boy still stretched out on the board that had been used to carry him from the saloon sobered their attitude to what they had to do. Neither man was a gunfighter but it was apparent to both that if they were going to confront Walt's killer their only hope of success was to do so when their blood was cooled.

So their next stop was the hotel where they secured a room for the night and discussed their strategy. Bart proposed that he should look for Clancy Jarrett alone. Al, he suggested, should stay out of any fight. Someone, he argued, had to get the supplies back to the cattle drive and pass on details of the events in Brannigan to Virgil Jefford. Al vetoed the idea. Whatever they did, they did together. It would be suicide for either of them to tackle Clancy Jarrett on his own. He was a killer and they were trail hands. Although neither of them was a stranger to death and violence, their experience with guns since the war was primarily in use against snakes and coyotes.

There were three saloons in town; Al and Bart visited each of them. No one they questioned admitted seeing Jarrett, or to having any knowledge of his whereabouts. As it was unlikely that Jarrett was in hiding from them, the cowboys came to the conclusion that either the sheriff had forbidden the citizens to inform them of Jarrett's whereabouts, or that simply, of their own volition, they didn't want to become involved in more blood-letting. The other possibility, of course, was that Jarrett was no longer in town. In the darkness relieved only by the weak light of the oil lamps that burned along the boardwalk of the near-empty street, that was the conclusion that Bart and Al slowly and reluctantly reached. Without assistance from the townspeople they had little choice but to return to their hotel rooms and, in the morning, return to the herd without achieving any justice for the death of Walt Dickers.

'We'll leave it to Mr Jefford,' said Al. 'He can decide what action is necessary, but I'm sure he'll consider our return with the provisions is our main objective. If he wants to come back here and hunt out Clancy Jarrett I'll be happy to accompany him.'

Although Bart's overriding desire for justice still urged him to seek out the missing slayer of young Walt Dickers, he offered no argument to Al. He knew as well as his older friend that Virgil Jefford wouldn't want them to put themselves in any danger. Already, he was running the herd with the minimum number of hands and there weren't many settlements on the trail to Cheyenne where new drovers could be hired. So Bart said nothing as they walked along the street.

Unknown to them, in the Red Garter, they had been separated from Clancy Jarrett and his cohorts by nothing more than a thin wood-panel wall. In a private room behind the saloon bar the outlaws had been eating the best fare in Brannigan. If withholding that fact from Al and Bart was, in some part, a gesture of repayment for their intervention during the stagecoach robbery, by far the greatest reason for the townsfolk's silence was self-preservation.

On too many occasions, at the slightest provocation, Clancy Jarrett had resorted to violence. They had little doubt that he wouldn't stop at killing the cowboys for interrupting his meal. Someone in the saloon would be slaughtered too, just to prove that Clancy Jarrett ruled the town.

On this occasion, however, the townsfolk were wrong. Clancy would have been delighted if Al and Bart had been directed his way. He was anxious to meet the other two cowboys who had foiled his attempted robbery, anxious to repay them as he had their young friend, but that confrontation had been avoided and, disappointed by their failure to find Jarrett, Al and Bart headed for the livery stable for a last check on the horses.

The call that attracted their attention was low, barely above a whisper, but on the near-empty street it carried to them with surprising clarity. It came from the alleyway that separated the Prairie Rose from the block that housed the millinery, the haberdasher's shop and the barber. Wary of a trap, the friends hesitated and studied the street. No one was close enough to witness anything that might occur. The call came again, accompanied by an impatient arm movement. With their hands on the butts of their revolvers they moved towards the alleyway.

The figure was pressed against the wall of the Prairie Rose, keeping to the shadow, making identification difficult. The person was not tall, was slight of build and wore a flat-crowned hat. 'It's a woman,' suggested Al, and when they reached the opening his assessment proved correct.

The saloon girl, Kate, spoke urgently, her bruised face lending weight to the tone of fear in her voice. 'I need help,' she said. 'I have to get to Billings. I can pay you if you'll ride with me tonight.'

Suspicious of the secretive manner of her approach, Bart wondered whether the girl was luring them into some sort of trap: was she distracting them for Clancy Jarrett's benefit? He told himself it would be foolish to think that her words were anything other than a rehearsed lie, but he couldn't believe that she was a good enough actress for the fire in her eyes to be anything but genuine fear. Still, by way of rejection, he said, 'We have to get back to our herd in the morning.'

'This is my only opportunity,' she cried, begging him now. From a dark canvas war bag at her feet she produced a small purse. Inside was a bundle of paper money. 'Please,' she repeated, offering the money to Bart.

Bart pushed her hand away. 'You must know many men in this town,' he said. 'Ask them.'

A brief, dismissive expression crossed her face but her urgency gave her little time for explanations. 'You are not afraid of Clancy Jarrett,' she said. 'Everyone else is.'

'It's not bravery, miss. Clancy Jarrett killed our partner and the law here seems unable or unwilling to do anything about it. It wouldn't be right to let Walt's death go unpunished. If the law won't do it, we have to try.'

'No,' she insisted. 'Don't try to fight him. He'll pull some trick to make sure you are killed and he survives. He won't fight fair. He doesn't fight fair. Not ever.' She thrust the money at him again. 'I know I haven't done anything to deserve your help,' she said. 'You think I should have told the sheriff that Clancy killed your friend without provocation. But I couldn't. Clancy has my sister. He'll kill her if I give him cause to, just as he'll destroy property and goods of anyone who threatens to stand up to him. Please help me. I have a chance to rescue Alice and ride away from here for ever.'

In the darkness Al and Bart exchanged looks, both wondering what kind of story the girl was attempting to spin to get them to help her.

'He has her at his cabin,' she continued. 'If I can get her away, we'll leave Brannigan for ever.'

Bart asked, 'What is she doing there?' The words were spoken even though he realized the futility of the question.

'He kidnapped her to punish someone else.' The anger hung heavily in Kate's voice.

How one man had been allowed to terrorize a town amazed Bart. 'Has anything been done to rescue her?'

Kate shook her head. 'Who would dare?' she said. 'And when he comes to town he usually leaves someone at the cabin to guard her.'

Bart's question had been aimed at finding out what had been done officially to investigate her sister's abduction: in particular, what Sheriff Oates had done to secure her release, but Kate's response gave him the answer: he'd done nothing. Bart's respect for the sheriff plummeted from not very high to nothing. No matter what restrictions had been imposed by the town committee, no honest lawman would permit such a crime to go unpunished.

'What makes you think there isn't a guard tonight?'

'Because Tulsa Jones and Sepp Minto came to Brannigan with Clancy, and it's all around town that Ollie Dent has left the territory. Gone south to Texas, some say.'

Al Dunnin grunted. He was thinking that if the rumours were right and the stagecoach had been held up by Clancy Jarrett and his partners, Ollie Dent might have been the one who had stopped his lead; he might be lying wounded in the shack where the girl's sister was being held.

Bart had similar thoughts but, for the moment, kept them to himself. His mind was more busily occupied, working on a bargain with the girl. They would help her if she would agree to testify to the fact that young Walt had been unlawfully killed. He put the proposition to Kate, but she was unwilling to agree, her reluctance based on her belief that Clancy Jarrett would never stand trial.

'Tell the facts to Sheriff Oates,' Bart told her. 'He'll have to arrest Jarrett.'

Kate shook her head. 'You don't realize how much power Clancy wields over this town. He'd have me killed before I could ever testify against him.'

'Then Al and I will get you and your sister to Billings,' decided Bart. 'There, you can tell your stories to the territorial marshal. He can make the arrest and keep you hidden until the trial.'

No matter what its rank or reputation, Kate didn't share Bart's faith in the efficacy of the law, but she needed help to rescue Alice. So, eventually, she showed her agreement by a movement of her head. By now she was impatient to be away and urged the two men to collect their horses. 'We must go now before Clancy and his men leave town,' she declared.

Al spoke. 'They might have done that already. We can't find them anywhere.'

'This is Clancy's horse,' said Kate, touching the saddle on a big dapple-grey tied to the hitching post outside the Prairie Rose. 'They haven't gone yet.'

Despite her plea for haste, there was gear to collect

from the hotel and horses to gather from the livery stable. Al volunteered to saddle the beasts while Bart undertook the tasks at the hotel. Kate agreed to tag along with Bart but as the three stepped out of the shadow of the alley, a figure approached them along the boardwalk. Sheriff Oates was making a patrol of the main street. He reacted with surprising alertness to the sudden appearance of the three people from the shadows. It wasn't the fastest draw that Al and Bart had ever seen but the sheriff had filled his hand with his pistol with professional efficiency, the gun pointing at the group with unwavering menace.

'No need for that, Sheriff,' declared Bart.

Sheriff Oates regarded them with suspicion, as though there was something unnatural about the dance-hall girl being in the company of two cowboys, but perhaps it was the clothes she wore and the way she held the old war bag tight to her chest.

'Kate,' began Bart, feeling a little uneasy at using her given name but ignorant of any other, 'is willing to testify against Clancy Jarrett. We're going to Billings to report to the territorial marshal. You can expect us back with him in a day or two to arrest Jarrett for murder. Unless you want to do it yourself?'

Sheriff Oates examined the faces of the people before him, clearly doubting the likely success of their mission. 'Hope you know what you're doing, Kate,' he said, giving her a meaningful look.

'She does,' said Bart. 'Perhaps in the morning you'll tell the fellow at the mercantile and the undertaker that we'll be back in a couple of days.'

The group split up, Al heading for the stable, Bart and Kate towards the hotel and the sheriff on his route to the far end of the quiet street. None of them saw Tulsa Jones who had stepped outside the Prairie Rose and, in the shadow of the veranda, had overheard the brief conversation. When the street was clear he crossed it quickly, anxious to pass on what he'd heard to Clancy Jarrett.

Clancy Jarrett was at a card table in the Red Garter when Tulsa found him. Clancy was grinning because he was winning. He was winning because Hank Pardoe and Dewey Shillitoe, whose game he'd intruded upon, were as nervous playing poker with him as a reverend having tea with the madam of a brothel.

Tulsa whispered his news urgently into Clancy's ear. 'Kate's got some cowboys to take her to Billings. She told Sheriff Oates that'll she testify against you to the marshal there.'

Clancy's grin broadened, amused that Kate thought she could get the better of him.

Tulsa took the smile from his face. 'She's got Jake Devane's war bag. The one he kept the money in. It didn't go into the river with the horse.'

Abruptly Clancy stood, his chair crashing to the floor behind him; the table was jolted by his thighs, scattering the coins, cards and drinks that were on it. Hank Pardoe and Dewey Shillitoe jumped to their feet, startled by the madness that showed in Clancy's eyes, his expression a terrible portent. They knew that whatever happened next would involve fearful violence. For a moment they were motionless; then, at his beckoning, they followed him and Tulsa outside. En route, Clancy attracted the attention of Sepp Minto, his rough call forcing his acolyte to join them and, in so doing, leave behind the manifold charms of a young Mexican girl.

'She was over by the Prairie Rose,' Tulsa explained, 'clutching Jake Devane's bag so tightly it had to hold more than her frills and ribbons. Sheriff Oates was there, too.'

It didn't cross Clancy Jarrett's mind for a moment that Tulsa could be wrong in his identification of Jake Devane's canvas bag. Jake had brought it every time they'd shared out the money from the stagecoach robberies. They all knew it, they had all joked about it. All that occurred to Clancy at that moment was that even in his last moments Jake had duped him, had led him to believe that the money had gone into the river with Alice and the horse. A red mist of fury filled Clancy's mind, which boded ill for Tom Oates who was, at the moment, approaching the Red Garter at the end of his patrol.

It took little more than a glance for Sheriff Oates to recognize Clancy Jarrett and even the approaching night couldn't hide the threat contained in the stance he'd adopted. His legs were slightly parted, like a prize-fighter's, settling on a firm foundation from which to launch an attack. His arms were bent so that his hands were across his stomach allowing his thumbs to be hooked into his gunbelt. He waited and watched the lawman's approach.

From the two-step-high boardwalk he looked down on the sheriff. 'Come to arrest me?'

Sheriff Oates couldn't miss the venom in Clancy's tone. It wasn't unusual for him to be goaded by the gunman but this time, somehow, there was a more immediate menace in his words. 'Just patrolling the town, like I do every night.'

'Thought perhaps you were here to save Kate a ride to

Billings. Thought perhaps you had an idea you could save the marshal a trip.'

Sheriff Oates didn't know how Clancy had obtained his information but, from the way Tulsa Jones shuffled uncomfortably two steps behind, it seemed clear that he had something to do with it. 'If Kate wants to involve the marshal that's her privilege.'

'Her privilege!' The words were uttered in disbelief, as though the sheriff had just declared that whiskey had been banned from Cheyenne to the Canadian border. Then Clancy laughed. 'Are you a gambling man, Sheriff? Because I'm prepared to bet that Kate never reaches Billings.'

For three years Tom Oates had been sheriff of Brannigan, had accepted the job because it was a quiet little town, a settled community of businesses and farm land. It was well away from the cow trails and had nothing to attract roistering cowboys that other settlements couldn't better provide. Other than a handful of incidents when punches had been thrown and property damaged, the cells had been little used. Then Clancy had arrived in town and from the first moment it had become clear to Oates that one day he would have to decide whether to stand up to him or ride away from Brannigan for ever.

'You leave that girl alone,' he said, his voice strong, challenging, expressing a greater confidence than he felt. 'This is my town, Clancy. There'll be no more murders here.'

The anger that had gripped Clancy since his arrival in Brannigan gave vent in reckless words. 'She'll never leave this town alive. I'll make her plead and beg first, just as I did with her sister. But it'll do no good. Nobody is going to put me in prison.'

The implication behind Clancy's words struck Sheriff Oates. 'Alice! You've killed her sister?'

'Prove it,' sneered Clancy.

Tom Oates didn't know where his courage came from. Perhaps it was anger brought about by Clancy's open disdain of the law and himself, or perhaps it was the realization that this was his moment of destiny. That now he had to be the lawman he'd pretended to be for three years. 'I want your gun.'

'Do you think you can take it?'

'I can try.'

'Then try now.'

Both men had reached for the pistols at their sides but Tom Oates never got his clear of his holster. Clancy's first shot knocked the sheriff off his feet. The outlaw stepped down into the road and fired a second into the dying lawman. He muttered some words over the body, mean words, disparaging of the man and his office, boosting his own masculine worthiness to such a degree as to render his opinion of the dead lawman no greater than the worms which would soon be at work on his body. He would have put another bullet in his victim but Tulsa Jones and Sepp Minto bundled him into an alleyway.

'That's enough,' Tulsa said. He had seen the faces of those who'd witnessed the killing, could hear the shock and anger that the deed had generated. Tom Oates might not have been the bravest sheriff west of the Missouri, but he had been their sheriff. Before another day dawned a telegram would be on its way to the county sheriff. He could hear the death knell marking the passing of Clancy

Jarrett's reign of violence. 'We've got to get out of town. Quickly.'

For the second time that day Al Dunnin was in the livery stable when he heard a gunshot. He had saddled three horses, using Walt's for the girl because it was a placid beast.

'Clancy Jarrett must still be in town,' the stableman said, spelling out to Al that Brannigan would be a decent place if Clancy Jarrett would stay away. Al left some coins with the man to cover the cost of stabling for the pack animals until he returned.

There was activity on the street as he walked his horse towards the hotel, holding the lead reins of the other two. The movement of the few people he could see in the dim glow of the lanterns had that awkward gait of despair. As he approached he heard a voice shout. 'It's the sheriff. He's dead.'

In the alleyway, Tulsa and Sepp were trying to persuade Clancy to head back to their shack, but Clancy was still not in control of his anger. 'Not until I've killed her and those cowboys. If they hadn't interfered none of this would have happened.'

At that moment Al came abreast of the little huddle of men. There was a body on the ground. A rifle lay close by. Sheriff Oates had looked anxious when speaking to Al and Bart only fifteen minutes earlier, but the cowboy doubted that it had been in anticipation of his own death. Up the street, he could make out Bart and the girl waiting on the hotel veranda. Al pricked the horse with his spurs to hurry it past the group just as the words of another voice carried to him.

'That's one of them,' Sepp Minto said, recognizing Al

as he rode slowly up the street with two unridden horses in his wake. Instantly, Clancy drew and fired.

Al experienced a searing sensation across his shoulders. He jerked upright, his eyes closed, then his back arched, but the instinct for survival took command of his actions and he threw himself forward along his horse's neck and again tapped its flanks with his spurs. Gripping the reins of the trailing animals he raced up the street. Another shot fired in his direction passed close over his head.

Clancy stepped into the street, firing more shots after the fleeing cowboy, but in an instant his fire was being returned.

As soon as he realized that Al was the gunman's target, Bart had run to his friend's assistance, Colt in hand, firing twice at those further along the street. Those citizens who had gathered to verify for themselves that the body in the street was that of their sheriff, now scattered to the relative safety of the boardwalks on either side of the street.

'Ride,' Bart yelled as Al rode by. Then, collecting the dropped reins of the two horses, he returned to where Kate waited.

More pistols shots came from their assailants but the darkness of the night failed their accuracy. While Kate mounted one of the horses, Bart returned their fire. Then a rifle sounded. The bullet came close and smacked into a stanchion of the hotel porch, slicing off a splinter which gouged a line in Bart's cheek. He fired another shot but his accuracy in the gloom was no better than that of his opponents, besides which, he didn't know who his enemies were: only that most of the people in that direction were innocent bystanders.

Bart wiped at the trail of blood on his cheek. His main

impulse was to go up the street and face those who were shooting at him. One of those, he knew, would be Clancy Jarrett, and making him pay for the death of young Walt Dickers still filled his thoughts. But now he had the girl to think about, had her sister to rescue and had to get them both to Billings so that Jarrett could answer to the law for all his crimes.

Kate was riding away now, looking back over her shoulder to see what was happening to Bart. He was in the saddle, yelling to her to ride hard and urging his own horse onward towards the end of the street. As he came level with the Prairie Rose he was aware of faces at the batwing doors and silhouetted against the glass of the windows. He was also aware of the horses tied to the hitching rail. He remembered Kate pointing out Clancy Jarrett's horse. He pulled his horse to a stop near the rail, unleashed the big dapple-grey and the three next to it and chased them out of town ahead of him. It might prevent immediate pursuit, might give them an extra few minutes to effect the rescue of Kate's sister.

CHAPTER FOUR

Lariat was one of those towns that had sprung up overnight to satisfy a specific need, had seen a couple of years of bustling, often violent frontier life, then had been abandoned to the elements when its purpose was at an end. Some such settlements had marked the progress of the railroad; around them the whiskey sellers, gamblers and whores had set up business to separate the line-layers from their money, only for each camp to be abandoned as the railroad progressed and a new base was established further west. But most, including Lariat, had been mining settlements, communities that had developed around a sudden strike of gold or silver. When that mineral petered out, the people moved on to their next El Dorado, their dreams packed on the back of a mule alongside their sifting pans, pickaxe and spade.

Once deserted, these towns quickly fell into disrepair. Untended timbers, warped and rotted by the alternate ravages of a burning sun and a furious storm, were soon spread across the land as the buildings succumbed to the strength of the prairie winds.

Hec Masters, who'd reined in his bay gelding on the

ridge above the town, looked down on the weed-strewn streets and counted the number of wood-frame buildings which had begun to buckle under nature's constant pressure. He recalled the words of his friend, Governor Sheedy. An unlived-in town, he'd stated in stentorian tones, lost its glamour quicker than an ageing whore. Hec chuckled at the memory. He wasn't sure how many ghost towns Grover Sheedy had seen, but he was certainly a world authority on whores.

But Lariat wasn't completely deserted. The building at the near end of town was still in use, a sort of tavern where a traveller could avail himself of small rations and ammunition, or perhaps a beer and a meal, or even a room for the night and feed for his horse. These things were available at a price and a traveller might even enjoy a hand of poker, for sometimes range hands from the surrounding ranches would ride in to break the monotony of the bunkhouse. But such irregular trade wasn't the purpose of the tavern. Its owner, the last man in Lariat, was a burly Swede called Ove Pettersen. He had been commissioned by the Friar Stage Line to maintain a way station there, it being a prime location for changing horses on the route between Missoula and Billings. Meals were prepared for the passengers and accommodation made available in an emergency. A fever had taken Ove's wife eight months earlier and now he did all the work himself.

Beyond the tavern building Hec could see more than a dozen horses in a corral. A big string was needed to cope with a daily stage in each direction. Hec could also see four saddle horses tied to the rail at the front of the building. Cowboys, he supposed, washing the dust from their throats after a day herding cattle. Before riding down to join them, Hec removed the badge from his shirt, read the inscription: US Marshal, which was embossed on it, then put it in his pocket. No need to advertise his profession. Sometimes people didn't talk easily to a lawman.

The room was big but, despite the three large windows in the front wall, it was gloomy and unfriendly, the bare walls and floor suggesting coldness even though summer was not yet over. Opposite the door a long counter ran almost the length of the room. Behind it an open door led through to another room. Several tables covered the floor space with hard wooden seats clustered around each, but at the end of the room nearer the street door, there were two long, deep-seated, leather covered settees, giving the establishment pretensions of being a hotel foyer. A stairway, hidden from the room by shabby wooden panels, led to an upper floor.

Three men sat around a table near the centre of the room, looking up as Hec pushed open the door. The oldest, a heavyset man whose face had been a stranger to a razor for several days, seemed to register surprise at Hec's entrance, but the marshal knew the reaction to be false for a fourth man, positioned at a window, had watched his approach from a long way out. Without advancing into the room, Hec studied the four faces. He was certain that he hadn't met any of the men before, yet there was something in the expression of the oldest man that made Hec uneasy; something in the way the head tilted when he faced him, as though he'd asked a question and was waiting for a response. His constant smile aggravated Hec because of its lack of conviction. Far better be like his companions, the marshal thought, whose morose expressions were almost open threats to his safety.

All four were dirty: not the dustiness of drovers who'd been twelve hours in the saddle, but grimy, like men who had been too long apart from civilization. Their clothes were old and stained as though they'd slept and travelled in them for several months, their hats were battered and black with sweat where they nestled on the brow. Their hands and be-whiskered faces were ingrained with dirt, emphasizing that they were as careless of their appearance as they were of other people's opinion.

'Come in, stranger,' greeted the oldest man of the four. 'If it's victuals you're after, you're just in time. The man back there is serving up a stew that smells mighty fine.'

Hec Masters could find no argument with that statement. The aroma that was travelling through from the back room was certainly mouth-watering. He walked across to the counter, conscious that the other men in the room watched every step, as though his arrival was an unwanted event, a precursor to disaster.

Ove Pettersen emerged from the back room carrying before him a large wooden tray on which there were four huge plates, each brimful with the tempting fare. He gave silent acknowledgement to Hec's presence. The man at the window left his post and took his place at the table alongside his companions. Ove made another trip to the back room, returning this time bearing bread and coffee. While the four men attacked the food provided, Ove turned his attention to Hec Masters.

'I've no more rooms,' he stated, pre-empting any such request from the marshal.

'Stopped by for a meal,' Hec told him. 'Hadn't decided whether or not I'd done travelling for the day but I reckon you've just made the decision for me.'

The man at the table arrested the journey of a spoon to his mouth. 'Too bad,' he called. 'Day's all but done. Always risky riding at night. Horse snaps a leg in a gopher hole and a man can find himself afoot in the wilderness. Might be days before he comes across another living soul.'

Hec acknowledged the man's words with a shrug. Such a catastrophe was possible in daylight. It was an automatic consideration for anyone who travelled alone in these parts, but hardly worth the mention to a trail-hardened Westerner like himself. He tried to read something more in the man's words or his facial expression, but his attention was once again on the food on his plate so Hec placed an order with the way-station man.

'If there's any left,' he said, 'I'll have a plate of that stew.'

For a moment it seemed that Ove Pettersen was going to refuse the order, his blue eyes holding the gaze of Hec Masters with a candid warning. Hec glanced over his shoulder once more but the four men gathered at the table were showing little interest in anything but the food before them. He took a table at the end of the bar and waited for his meal to be served.

Later, as the group of four were finishing their meal, the older man, their spokesman, wiped his plate clean with a wedge of bread and called across the room to Hec. 'I was thinking, one of the deserted buildings might provide you with a more comfortable bedding place than the open hills. Never know when a storm will break at this time of year. Continue your journey in the morning. In daylight.'

'Sleeping in the open doesn't bother me,' Hec replied. 'Besides, I can get two hours further along the trail before it gets too dark to travel.'

'You got far to go?'

'Far enough,' replied Hec.

The old man laughed. It was a wheezing sound meant to show his respect for Hec's cautious response. 'The minute you walked through that door I knew you were a good-living, God-fearing man, like myself. A man of purpose, capable of taking care of his own business without the need of help or advice from anyone who crosses his trail. I meant no offence by my enquiry, merely offering to share our company with a lonesome traveller.'

'No offence taken,' said Hec.

'Then perhaps you'll take a hand of cards with us before you travel on. Gus here,' he indicated the man on his left, the one who had been over by the window, 'is such a bad poker player that I feel guilty taking his money. Harv's pappy was a preacher,' he added with a nod in the direction of the man who sat opposite. 'Told him the Devil invented gambling, that it is a sin, so he won't tolerate it. No sir.'

Hec assessed Harv with one casual look. If he didn't gamble it was the only sin in which he didn't participate. Like Gus and the remaining man his expression was without warmth or humour. They were men who had no permanent home, no anchor in their lives, the owners of the sort of cruel, cold-eyed faces that he'd studied on a hundred Wanted posters.

The old man introduced himself as Cyrus and the remaining man as Nate. Cyrus claimed he'd already taken most of Nate's money, which meant that it was hardly worth playing with him again. Nate didn't smile when he turned to face Hec, but neither had Harv or Gus. However, Hec's own demeanour had not been effusive, but nor had it been surly or aggressive. He'd adopted a detached manner, watching and listening, giving himself the opportunity to gather information and assess the character of each man in the room.

As he took his place at the table the marshal introduced himself simply as Hec. Harv moved away, taking the station by the window. Cards were obtained from Ove Pettersen and a game chosen. Despite the older man's disparaging remarks, Gus and Nate were dealt in.

'Couldn't help but notice your iron.' Cyrus spoke while Hec skipped the cards over the table. 'Mr Colt makes some very fine weapons. That's one of his Peacemakers, I believe.'

'It is.'

'Judging by the smoothness of the walnut I'd say that one has been well used.'

Hec raised his eyes from the cards to look into those of Cyrus. The old man chuckled, a defensive sound, as though acknowledging that he had strayed into a stranger's personal territory but suggesting that it was an innocent trespass. When he spoke again, his tone was placatory.

'A man only survives in this country if he can take care of himself. Your gun is a confirmation of my earlier observation. You are, I believe, a man of great determination.'

Determination was a description which sat easily with Hec Masters, and part of that determination meant that he, too, observed people but the facts obtained he kept to himself. For instance, he, too, noticed the guns men carried, not just the make but the manner of wearing

61

them, whether a man was ill at ease with the weight of the iron on his hip, or whether he carried it in a high hip-holster attached to his belt or in a gunbelt, low on his thigh. To these men, a gun was as essential as a hat in the noon sun. Although he didn't know their faces he had no doubt that somewhere they were sketched on a Wanted poster.

As the game progressed Hec Masters became more uncomfortable. Harv had strayed from the window and had taken up a post somewhere to his rear, out of sight. Only the old man spoke but his often flowery speech failed to hide a threatening tone. As the light outside began to dwindle the more aware Hec became that violence was close at hand.

Hec laid down two queens and two tens and proceeded to scoop the coins from the table. 'Time to go,' he declared, rising to his feet as he stuffed the money into his pocket.

The old man protested. 'You've got to give us a chance to win back our money.'

Hec shook his head. 'I've stayed here too long. There's a good hour of travelling time left in the day. I mean to take advantage of it.'

The men around the table began moving, shuffling to their feet as though in anticipation of departure themselves. Ove Pettersen called to Hec Masters. 'Six bits you owe me.'

Hec produced the coins as he reached the counter. 'Six?'

'I gave your horse a feed bag,' Ove explained. 'Moved him round to the water trough at the back. Come, I'll show you.'

Hec tipped his hat at the men with whom he'd played cards. 'So long,' he told them then followed Ove out through the door behind the counter, into the room where the food was prepared and beyond that into the cool of the evening.

In a low voice Ove asked, 'You're a marshal?' Hec nodded his head in agreement. 'Those men,' Ove continued, 'they know you. The one at the window recognized you when you rode in. They mean you trouble. That's why I didn't want you to stay. Go. Go quickly. I've moved their horses, too.'

'Who are they? Do you know?'

'No. But it seems you killed the old man's son.'

Hec hurried in Ove's wake. It wasn't fear that urged him to rush away from the tavern but a reluctance to start on a path that would lead to more death. If he rode away that might be the end of the matter, their paths might never cross again. That was his hope, deep down he knew the reality was something different. But he was already on an official mission and was reluctant to have it interrupted by another man's grudge.

The noise that alerted them to their follower could have been a dragged foot on the wooden floor or a the scrape of a leg as a chair was moved aside. Hec was still trying to summon up a face, one that the brief similarity had hinted at when he'd first studied the old man, but now, with the furtive sound from within still sharp, he had more pressing business to handle. As he reached his horse he removed his hat and hung it on the roping horn on his saddle. Then, crossing behind the animal, he stepped into the shadow of the high corral gatepost. Virtually invisible, he waited for his tracker.

But the first person he saw didn't come from the rear of the tavern, Nate, an unmistakably lanky character, eased his way around the corner from the front. He edged forward, keeping to the shadows, thinking himself concealed because he didn't know he'd already been observed. When Harv emerged from the rear door he paused and looked across to the corral where Ove Pettersen still stood. In a moment he caught Nate's signal: a twist of his gun to urge him forward towards Ove and the corral, moonlight glinting off its barrel.

Quietly, slowly, without betraying his location, Hec Masters lowered himself into a crouch. Cautiously, gun at the ready, Harv approached. Hec whispered to Ove. 'Come closer. Slowly.' The way station owner obeyed, moving backwards, as if retreating in fear from Harv.

'Where is he?' Harv's query wasn't loud but the coarseness of his voice betrayed his apprehension and confusion. By now he was almost at the gate but his gaze was fixed on Ove.

Ove took another step back, then another, his legs now hiding Hec completely. One more step. Then he stopped and pointed towards the hills beyond the tavern. 'Gone,' he said, taking another step back so that the marshal had room to rise. Harv had turned to look in the direction that Ove pointed, thus presenting the back of his head to Hec and against which Hec crashed the barrel of his Colt. Harv fell senseless to the ground.

'Hey,' called Nate. The distance between him and the corral was such that he couldn't clearly discern the activity in the gateway, but he knew that the commotion followed by the thud as Harv hit the ground were significant to the hunt for the US marshal.

Ove Pettersen was taking further steps away from Hec Masters as the marshal called to Nate. 'Put down your gun.'

Nate did the opposite, convinced that the shadows in which he hid were sufficient cover against any attack that the marshal might be considering. He fired once, the bullet screaming away into the night, spooking the horses in the corral. Hec Masters fired his own gun, holding back the trigger and fanning the hammer twice. Both shots hit their target. Nate sprawled in the dust, dead before his knees had begun to buckle under his weight.

Footsteps, running, sounded from the side of the building. 'Did you get him, Nate?' asked Cyrus as he came around the corner.

Hec's retort was spoken slowly, clearly, so that Cyrus and the trailing Gus stopped in their tracks. 'No, he didn't. Now drop your guns.' To ensure that they adhered to his instruction, Hec fired a shot over their heads. 'Now step away from them,' he ordered. 'Come this way. Into the moonlight so that I can see you.'

'Where's my boy?' asked Cyrus.

'If you mean Nate, he's in the dust over there. Dead. If you mean Harv, he's lying here with a cracked skull. Now you two lie down, stretch wide your arms and legs and eat dirt.' To Ove Pettersen he said, 'Collect all the guns and bring me their horses.'

While the Swede did as he was asked, Hec Masters mounted his own horse and rode over to where the two men lay on the ground. It was impossible for them to look up into the marshal's face; answering his questions was difficult enough.

'Who are you?' Hec asked.

'Cyrus Tobin,' said the old man. 'You killed my eldest boy.'

'Zach Tobin.' Hec remembered the man and recognized the likeness around the mouth and chin that was apparent in the father. 'I didn't kill your son. He was legally executed. Tried, found guilty of robbery and murder and hanged.'

'Hanged because of you,' Cyrus Tobin spat out. 'What kind of death is that for a man? Kicking for air on a gallows.'

'It's the death prescribed by law. He took the risk and paid the penalty.'

'And what's the penalty for the likes of you, Hec Masters? It'll be death just the same when I catch you.'

'You let it go now, Tobin. You've already got one more man killed and another with a lump on his head the size of the Rocky Mountains. Now I've got some business to take care of so I'm taking your horses and your guns. I'll leave them a mile or two along the trail. Don't you go taking a notion to follow. I don't want to have to kill you but I will if I need to. Stay on the ground until I'm over that ridge, then you can see to Harv.'

Hec took the reins offered to him by Ove Pettersen. The gunbelts, he saw, were hung over one of the saddle horns. He tipped his hat and rode away. True to his word, he left the horses a couple of miles from the tavern and flung the guns in different directions to add to the annoyance of their owners. In addition, in case Cyrus Tobin harboured thoughts of tracking, Hec left the horses on the high trail that led to Missoula and doubled back to the low valley trail, which would get him to his destination in two days. He rode for almost two hours, longer than had been his intention and later than was his usual practice, but both he and his horse were well fed and the farther he got from Cyrus Tobin the happier he would be.

CHAPTER FIVE

At about the time Hec Masters was bedding down, Al, Bart and Kate were approaching the shack used by Clancy Jarrett and his men. With the reports of more than one firearm behind them, they'd left Brannigan at a flat run, the descending darkness sufficient to make the accuracy of their attackers little more than a matter of chance. Nonetheless, they'd ridden hard, determined to create between themselves and any pursuers as great a gap as possible. They were almost two miles beyond the town limits when they pulled off the trail and drew rein to take stock of the situation. Here, the land was open but undulating, rising in a series of smooth mounds to an uneven horizon, and among those hillocks were deep, shadow-filled hollows in which a rider was as difficult to see as bats in a cave.

They sat in one of these natural depressions for half a minute, in silence, listening for hoofbeats or any other sound of pursuit. None came; all they heard were the snorts of their own mounts and the rattle of their own harnesses. With a signal for the others to remain, Bart rode slowly back to the top of the low mound they'd recently descended and from there surveyed their back trail. The position he'd chosen was well below the horizon and in the fast descending gloom he was confident he would not be easily observed by a hard-riding tracker. He watched for several moments until he was satisfied that Jarrett and his men were not in the immediate vicinity. The need to find the scattered horses had, it seemed, given them the hoped-for advantage.

His next concern was the injury to Al Dunnin. Al was holding himself awkwardly, as though being astride a horse was a new experience, anxious that it might take flight and him without the know-how to stop it. When Bart asked how serious it was, Al told him it stung like hell but he'd suffered worse in the past. Bart examined the wound. Al had been lucky. The bullet had ripped through his shirt, had seared a line upwards, across his back and over his left shoulder. There wasn't a great deal of blood but the skin around was pink, swollen and had begun to smart. It looked like a single whiplash. With his knife Bart cut away a section of Al's shirt to prevent irritation.

'Haven't got time to do more at the moment,' he told his friend, 'I'll tend to it when we get further away from town.'

Kate spoke, her words surprising both men.

'We have to go back.'

Before either of them could think of the right question to ask in reply, Kate explained. 'We're going in the wrong direction. We're heading east, which will get us to Billings where the county sheriff and territorial marshal are based, but first we need to rescue my sister. I'm not sure of the exact location of Clancy Jarrett's shack but I know it is to the west of Brannigan.'

'That may be so,' said Al, 'but we can't go back.'

'What Al means,' Bart told her, preventing the argument which her expression now forecast, 'is that we can't go back the way we came. We have to loop around the town to avoid anyone who might be in pursuit.'

What Kate knew about Jarrett's cabin was that it was sited close to the Hollowhorn, a stream that came down from the Bitterroots and looped south of Brannigan before merging with the Dearborn, further east.

'The Hollowhorn,' she declared, 'is twenty minutes away.' She pointed south, to the horizon below which they sat, indicating that the Hollowhorn was beyond the heights. 'If we follow the river it shouldn't take us more than an hour to find the cabin.'

In territory that was unknown to them, Al and Bart had little option other than to adopt the girl's plan. The drawback was the need to cross the skyline to reach the river. Bart's recent surveillance had shown no sign of pursuit so it was agreed that the quicker they undertook the crossing the lower their risk of discovery.

'Al,' Bart said, 'why don't you head back to the cattle? Report to Mr Jefford.'

'We've already had this discussion,' said Al. 'We stick together. I can't go back to Brannigan to collect the provisions and I can't go back to Mr Jefford without them.'

There was no need for any more discussion. Bart headed his horse towards the incline and, in Indian file, Kate and Al followed. They didn't hurry over the skyline, judging, instead, that a sedate pace was less likely to catch the eye of anyone below. Indeed, they crossed over without any indication that they had been seen or that there were any pursuers in the vicinity. Beyond, between themselves and the narrow ribbon of water that was the Hollowhorn, a cover of trees stretched along the river-bank, providing hope that they would be able to travel swiftly and avoid detection.

The big moon provided good illumination and they were able to keep the horses at a steady pace. By keeping to the river side of the tree line they were confident of trav-elling unobserved. The tree cover held good most of the way and it was only when they reached a sweeping bend in the river that the land opened up to the sort of rolling grassland that had brought cattle ranching to Montana. But even though they were then more exposed their journey passed without incident. Al estimated they'd trav-elled eight miles when they spotted the silhouette of the cabin high above the water's edge. To Al and Bart it looked little better than some of the line shacks on Virgil Jefford's range, but Kate insisted that it had to be Clancy's cabin. There was no internal glow of lamplight and no external indication of horses or other livestock close at hand.

'Are you sure this is the place?' Al asked.

'It's got to be.' Kate's voice carried a reedy quality, a sign of her concern at the apparent abandonment of the place, but she qualified her answer by assuring the cowboys that other landowners in these parts had substan-tial ranch houses and outbuildings.

'Come on then,' said Bart. He dismounted and led the way cautiously forward, each of them covering his horse's muzzle to prevent it betraying their approach. Twenty yards from the house they paused by a cluster of wild blue-berry bushes. They waited and watched but there was no indication that the premises were in use.

71

'Alice must be asleep,' said Kate, but it was clear that she, too, was aware of the desolation surrounding the place. It bore an atmosphere of abandonment.

'Are you sure this is the right place?' asked Al.

Her eyes shone with black anger at his doubt. 'Yes,' she hissed, but deep down she knew she doubted her own insistence.

'Wait here,' Bart told her. With a head motion he indicated for Al to follow.

They approached stealthily, guns in hand, reaching the building and pressing their ears to the wood-plank walls to listen for noises from within. Nothing. Al, still cautious lest the outlaw he'd wounded during the stagecoach robbery was within, indicated that he would walk around the shack for signs of occupancy. It took less than two minutes before he was back, standing across the doorway from his partner. He'd looked through the windows he'd passed and was now convinced that the place was empty. Keeping his gun ready, he pushed open the door.

Al stepped inside, quickly moving to one side so that he didn't make an easy target in the doorway. But no shots were fired and no one shouted a warning or in any way made their presence known. Bart entered close behind, taking up a position at the opposite side of the room to Al. After a few seconds of silence he called Alice's name but received no response. Eventually Al struck a match and shone it around the room.

Nothing about the inside improved its status from their first impression. A pot-bellied stove held central position and around it the furniture was unsubstantial and crude. Here and there around the room were two tables, four chairs, a cupboard and two up-and-down bunk beds, their blankets and pillows piled in disarray upon them. Assorted clothing hung on pegs and nails that had been affixed to the walls. A door led into a rear room and after putting a second match to a kerosene lamp Al went through to investigate. It, too, was empty and untidy.

Bart called to Kate, who came forward with the horses. 'No one here,' he told her, but she pushed past him as though he hadn't searched properly and her sister was just waiting for her to step into the shack before making an appearance. By the light of the single lamp held high by Al, Kate studied the room, her expectation of discovering her sister somewhere on the premises rapidly waning.

'Where's Alice,' she said, her voice low, as though hoping no one would hear her because she feared their answer.

'Perhaps this is the wrong cabin,' suggested Bart.

Alice shook her head. She'd recognized a heavy woollen coat that belonged to Ollie Dent and was pretty sure that Tulsa Jones owned the short boots that were under the bunk bed in the corner. 'This is Clancy's cabin,' she said, but her sister would never have lived among such disarray. Even though she had been brought to live here against her will, Kate knew that Alice wouldn't tolerate living in such squalor. Her sister was no fussy housewife but nor was she a drab who would leave unwashed pots around the place. 'Where is she?' she asked again.

Bart answered. 'I don't know, but we can't afford to hang around here wondering about it. Perhaps Jarrett isn't chasing a lost trail eastward. He might think he's scared us back to the cattle drive and is content that we've left Brannigan. He seems to have everyone else afraid of him so why should he think Al and I are any different?'

Mention of Al reminded Bart of his friend's wound. 'What we've got to do,' he continued, 'is to find some ointment for Al's back, then hit the trail for Billings. We need to report to the law officer there as soon as possible.'

If Kate wanted to argue about the brusque abandonment of her sister's rescue, and the tight-lipped expression on her face suggested she did, she managed to keep hold of the words. Much as she wanted to search high and low for Alice, she could find no fault with the cowboy's reasoning. It was apparent that Alice was no longer here and it was not to their benefit to dally. While Al held the lamp she searched the likely places for some sort of salve with which to dress his wound.

There was a drawer set into each end of the table. The first one they examined offered up nothing of assistance: an assortment of cutlery items, scissors, two hammers and box of nails. The contents of the other drawer were no more helpful in supplying their need but something caught Kate's eye and for a silent moment she gazed at it.

'What's the matter?' asked Al.

'That belt. It belongs to Alice.' A slim, soft leather belt lay in the drawer like a dead snake. Kate reached out a hand to touch it but withdrew it at the last moment, as though touching it would imply a false reverence. 'And that brooch,' she said, 'the cameo, that too, belonged to Alice.'

'She was here then,' said Al, not that he had ever doubted the fact but he knew that this find put a new slant on the fate of the girl.

'Look.' Kate picked up another item and held it out. In her hand she held a pearl-handled derringer. 'This belongs to Jake Devane.'

Bart, who had been collecting a clean shirt from Al's saddle-bag, joined them. 'Who is Jake Devane?'

'A gambler. A gambler with plans to open a saloon. Alice was part of those plans.' She was silent for a moment, remembering her last conversation with Jake Devane. 'He told me he was going to rescue Alice but I didn't believe him. I thought he'd run out on her. Left her to her fate at the hands of Clancy and his men.'

'Seems he did. Or at least he tried.'

'They've killed him, haven't they,' she gasped. In that instant she realized the significance of his war bag; why he hadn't returned for it. When Jake Devane had left it with her she had assumed it held nothing more than the extra clothes he'd taken with him to Missoula. When he didn't return for it she believed he had been so gripped with fear that he had left town in too much of a hurry to bother about it. But, earlier that evening, having determined to quit Brannigan, she'd picked up the war bag to use for her own scant belongings.

However, when she'd opened it, she'd discovered a small fortune in paper money, much of it bundled in bank wrappers. She knew it must be the money Jake had intended to use to buy the Cheyenne saloon; his leaving it behind had puzzled her. Still, it was the first bit of luck that had ever befallen either herself or Alice, the realization of which had been the birth of her resolution to rescue her sister. Rescue accomplished, they would travel east and live in greater comfort than they had ever known in their lives. But the discovery of the derringer altered everything. It meant that Jake had tried to rescue Alice and had failed. 'They've killed Alice, too,' she said with a sigh.

'Which adds to the importance of reaching Billings,'

Bart declared. 'Clancy Jarrett needs to answer for his crimes.'

An unlabelled jar in a cupboard in the back room contained a greenish, jelly-like substance which might have been a salve meant just as much for horses as it was for men. Bart smeared it across Al's back and covered the wound with strips of his old shirt. Then they were back in the saddle, grateful that Jarrett and his men had not yet returned to the cabin.

This time they looped north of Brannigan, not only to avoid any trackers but also to make use of higher ground, giving them the advantage of spotting any activity on the trail below. Kate, her thoughts inward, followed in the wake of the two cowboys.

Clancy Jarrett and his men weren't an immediate threat to Bart, Al and Kate. By the time the horses had been recovered and brought back to Brannigan, the trio were already on the riverside trail towards the cabin. Clancy, his face dark with anger, had ridden out of town at breakneck speed and hadn't drawn rein until he was well past the point where his quarry had left the trail.

His anger sprang from several causes now. That the cowboys had escaped his guns was a source of humiliation to Clancy Jarrett; added to this was the insult of leaving him afoot in a town that was rapidly becoming hostile to him. It was an act that couldn't go unpunished. He wanted them dead. The events of the evening merely added to the resentment he already felt over the failure to secure the money from the stagecoach hold-up. The killing of the boy hadn't been sufficient to appease him, and nothing would, until his pockets were once again full of someone else's money. But the information that Tulsa Jones had brought to the Red Garter, that Kate, a saloon whore, not only intended giving evidence against him to a US marshal but was also in possession of Jake Devane's money, ignited a hatred in him that took control of his mind. He wanted that money and would do whatever was necessary to get it.

Hank Pardoe and Dewey Shillitoe, whose horses had been hitched outside the Red Garter, were dispatched to round up those that had been scattered. It wasn't a job they wanted. Their past was not crime free but it had no mark on it that came close to killing a sheriff. The fact that they had been on the boardwalk beside Clancy when he shot Tom Oates probably confirmed, in the eyes of the towns-people, their complicity with the deed. The trouble was that they had no more desire to be in Clancy's company than had any other citizen of Brannigan. From the first moment he'd intruded in their card game the dark thunder of his countenance had been a warning that he was not to be crossed. They had little doubt that in this mood he would kill anyone who disobeyed him.

So they brought back the scattered horses and rode out with him in pursuit of those he sought, riding for five miles or more before stopping at a fork in the trail. There were no clear tracks to follow; there hadn't been since leaving Brannigan; they had simply ridden pell-mell in the hope of catching their quarry before they got too far ahead. It was Tulsa who suggested they could have left the trail further back and taken to the high ground to make tracking difficult, but it was Sepp who brought up the pos-sibility that they had made for the cabin.

'Kate thinks you've still got her sister there. Perhaps

she's persuaded those cowboys to help free Alice. This Billings business might be nothing more than a ruse to get us racing in the wrong direction.'

Clancy could see some merit in Sepp's words. Perhaps they had gone to the cabin, but if they had they would now know the truth about Alice. Kate had sworn vengeance against him that afternoon when he'd slapped her around after killing the boy. Now, armed with the knowledge that her sister was no longer at the cabin, she would be all the more determined to reach Billings and tell everything to the law there.

'If they've gone to the cabin then they are some miles behind us. It's unlikely that they'll travel at night. All trails to Billings converge near the old Indian burial ground. If we get there first we'll have them trapped, and if we don't there ought to be some sign that they've passed and we'll press on and catch them.' He dismounted. 'We'll rest here a few hours but we'll make tracks again before sunup.'

CHAPTER SIX

Since leaving the cabin, Kate had scarcely spoken ten words. The discovery of her sister's death had taken the wind from her sails and she rode trancelike, as though entirely dependent upon the whim of her mount. In the absence of instruction, the horse was governed by its herding instinct. It ran close on the heels of the horse in front, eased to a halt in unison with the others and stood head to head with them while Bart and Al discussed travelling at night. It was a short conversation, the outcome almost foreseeable by the very fact that Bart had brought everyone to a halt. Although both cowboys cast glances in her direction, Kate's distress had little bearing on their decision to rest awhile.

It wasn't that they were weary or that their horses were tired, the remuda of Virgil Jefford's cattle drive comprised tough working ponies of proven endurance, but the practicality of the situation was that they were in territory that was unknown to either of them and, although they wanted to get the girl to Billings as quickly as possible, they couldn't afford to lose sight of the fact that there might be men searching for them.

Whatever it was that had triggered the outbreak of violence in Brannigan was a mystery to them, but the identification of Al as 'one of them' made it clear that they were the gunmen's target. Although they knew it was in their best interest to return to the cattle as soon as possible, they had first to think of the girl's safety. Stumbling around in the dark would not ensure that and occupation of the high ground would only be an advantage in daylight.

They carried little in the way of provisions, merely a couple of cans they'd found in Clancy Jarrett's shack. The biscuits they'd put in their saddle-bags that morning before leaving the herd had all been eaten on the journey to Brannigan. There was a slosh of now warm water in each of the canteens, still capable of washing away dust from mouth and throat but no longer able to refresh. Nor was there any chance of boiling it up to make coffee. Even though they'd sought the cover of a stand of tall pines, neither man suggested lighting a fire. The smallest glow on the hillside could betray their position to their pursuers.

Because the night air was chilly, Bart spread his blanket over Kate who lay on the ground, her head against a saddle. For three hours Al rested, too, then relieved Bart, whose hillside vigil had been undisturbed. Predawn, they were back in the saddle and by the time light and warmth was being provided by the rising sun, they had covered several miles.

The further they travelled, the more confident the cowboys became that they would reach Billings without any further contact with Clancy Jarrett. The slopes across which they rode were well-forested, obscuring their progress east from any riders on the lower trail. So far they hadn't seen any activity below, a fact that didn't surprise Bart.

The previous night, as they'd made their way towards Jarrett's cabin, he'd talked over the shooting of the sheriff with Al and the girl. Because Al had been the next target, they drew the conclusion that the sheriff had confronted Clancy Jarrett over the killing of Walt Dickers. There was no reason to suppose that Clancy had any knowledge of Kate's intention to reach Billings, nor, indeed, that he knew that she was the person who had ridden out of Brannigan with Al and Bart. In the gloom, dressed in pants and shirt and with her hair tucked away inside her hat, it would have been difficult enough to specify that the third person was a woman.

So, Bart mused, if Clancy Jarrett didn't know their true purpose in leaving town he had no reason to suspect them of being on this trail to Billings. Until it was known that Kate was the third rider, it would be natural for him to assume that Al and he were heading back to the cattle drive. No matter how angry Clancy was, chasing them in that direction would be too great a risk. He had no way of knowing how close the herd and other trail hands might be.

Al was leading the way, riding half a dozen strides ahead of Bart and Kate. The reluctance to communicate which had so enveloped the girl when they'd bedded down, still hung around her, but the sunshine of the new day seemed to have warmed out of her some of the hostility that had kept her silent. Although she'd had little sleep, the deso-late, pinched expression was now replaced with a pallid but resolute countenance, and her eyes, which had been

81

almost drained of their colour, now showed such darkness in the blue that Bart was prepared to attribute to it an unflinching resolve. It was clear that she was still troubled by the death of her sister, but just as clear that she had come to terms with the fact that life goes on. A need for revenge she openly displayed, but mourning had become a private matter.

Bart opened a conversation, figuring that getting the girl to talk would be a greater benefit to her than allowing her thoughts to steep in silence.

'What'll you do when you get to Billings?' He wondered if she knew people there, if there was anyone to help and house her.

'What'll I do?' she repeated, her voice rich with anger, her face showing hostility, as though his enquiry was a mockery of her circumstances.

Trying to ignore her reaction, Bart calmly explained his question. 'I wondered if you planned to stay on in Billings or if you had folks someplace that you were going to visit.'

Kate smirked. 'No folks,' she said. 'I'll just continue to do in Billings what I was reared to do.' She touched her heels to her horse's flanks and moved a few strides closer to Al, leaving Bart to wonder what sore spot he'd unknowingly touched.

It was beyond noon when Al brought the small party to a halt. Here, the slopes were bare of trees; only tough grasses and small plants grew low among the rocks, so sparse that there was little colour to the hillside. The day was hot and bright, and water, not much more than a constant trickle, was running off the high rocks on its course to join the river below. They dismounted, interrupted the water run with their hands, using what they caught to quench their thirst and wash themselves cool. Bart attended to the horses, letting them drink from his hat, while Kate replenished the canteens.

Al studied the trail below. An hour earlier he had thought he had seen movement, perhaps a horseman, perhaps more than one, but whatever had caught his eye had not reappeared and he was prepared to write it off as wildlife, a pronghorn or even a grizzly on a search for food. Even if it had been a horseman there was no reason to assume he was a threat, part of a posse hunting for them. The trail below was the main route to Billings. It would be unremarkable if someone was travelling it. But he hadn't said anything to the others and still it niggled at the back of his mind.

Al looked ahead. The distant sky looked black and ominous. A storm was in their path. Soon, they would need to find shelter while it passed over, a delay they could well do without. Al thought of the cattle further south. Storms spooked cattle almost as much as fire and if the one now approaching veered south then Virgil Jefford with his short-handed crew would have his work cut out to hold the beeves in check.

He was about to voice that thought to Bart Sween when something on the slopes almost a mile ahead caught his eye.

'What do you think that is, Bart?'

His companion let his gaze wander in the direction where Al's finger pointed and fixed on a shelf that was fifty feet below the summit. What at first sight appeared to be a large, derelict timber construction, materialized on closer inspection to be a series of individual platforms supported by poles. Al grunted and answered his own question. 'Indian biers,' he said, 'Probably Sioux holy ground.'

Kate joined the cowboys. 'How do you know?'

'Seen them before,' Al told her. 'Good spot. Overlooking the valley and the river to the far prairie.'

'Will it still be in use?'

Al shook his head. 'All Indians are on reservations. This territory is forbidden to them now. At one time there was probably a regular summer village down there in the loop of the river. Favourable spot for hunting. The buffalo route is less than a day south of here.'

Bart turned away, replacing his hat, happy to let the small amount of water unconsumed by the horses drizzle down his brow and neck. 'Come on,' he said, 'we need to keep moving.'

'Why don't you two rest up awhile?' Al said. 'The trail seems to descend here. Perhaps we have to rejoin the main route. I'll scout ahead. Make sure there are no *obstructions.*' He hoped the word obstructions would hide from the girl his concern that, if they were still being pursued, their hunters might be close at hand. By the sharp look that Bart threw in his direction he knew he hadn't fooled his friend. He climbed on to his horse and moved slowly, cautiously, down the trail.

The lower he descended, the more fertile the terrain became and the trail wound its way through an abundance of timber. He was aware that the forested lower slopes had, for the past hour, provided better cover for travellers on the valley trail than it had for himself and his companions high on the bare hillside. There was no longer any doubt that the trail they were using descended all the way to the foot of the high ground where it would merge with the main route. If they'd been seen on the hillside then anyone who knew this territory would be aware that they had to descend at this point, making it a likely spot for an ambush.

The grass and flora grew thick enough to deaden the sound of the fall of his horse's hoofs. Even so, such was the sense of danger which gripped Al that when he was fifty feet from the point where the downward path merged with the valley trail he dismounted and tethered his mount among the pines. His cautious progress was not prompted by anything he'd observed from above but by his gut instinct. Wartime experiences had proved to him the benefit of scouting ahead; seeking out telltale warnings and sloppy ambushes. A few minutes sacrificed for advance reconnaissance could save hours on a post-battle burial detail.

It was a movement that first alerted him to the presence among the foliage. It was so slight and uncorroborated for so long that Al began to think that he had been fooled by his own tension and imagination. Then a rustling sound and a cough reached him, the noises no more than twenty paces from where he stood. Silently, he moved among the trees, circling the position he'd marked, a manoeuvre which took him further down the hillside until he could see the wider valley trail and the point where the routes merged. The advantages of that site as a point of ambush were immediately obvious. All around, trees and rocks provided not only suitable vantage points from which to catch the victim in crossfire, but also cover against any return shots.

Al waited patiently, three minutes, hoping that any cohorts of the man he'd discovered would also betray their position so that he would know how many lay in wait. But, although he suspected there were other men close by, the only creature he saw was the man's saddle horse standing quietly a dozen paces from its owner. Al moved cautiously, anxious that the beast didn't betray his presence but, apart from turning its head in his direction and pricking up its ears, it demonstrated no interest in him. Even so, Al couldn't afford to dawdle. Bart and the girl, either impatient of waiting or curious about his delayed return, might ride down the hill and into the ambush. Prompted by this possibility he made his move.

Dewey Shillitoe, the man Al had pinpointed among the trees, held his rifle in both hands, his attention fixed on a boulder across the trail behind which lay Clancy Jarrett. Although he had no heart for this job Dewey was determined not to miss any signal from Clancy, knowing that to do so would incur his anger. Clancy was sure that this ambush would be a success but Dewey hoped he was wrong. He hoped that those men were either not using this trail or else riding hell for leather for Billings and beyond their reach. When he got back to Brannigan, he'd decided, he would persuade Hank Pardoe that it was time for them to pack their gear and head for another territory. This was the thought in his mind when the gun barrel was pressed tightly above his right ear and his rifle was taken from him. A voice whispered in his ear. 'Who are you waiting for?'

'What do you mean?' That was Dewey's best attempt to appear innocent but all it earned him was the pressure of the gun being pushed harder against his skull so that his head tilted dramatically to the left. 'Some cowboys,' he blurted, but instinct told him to keep his voice at whisper level.

The angle at which Al held his gun at Dewey's head aggravated his own wound, giving rise to a sensation that the skin was tearing apart; that any healing that had begun with the application of the ointment at Clancy's cabin had been totally undone. To the best of his ability, he ignored it.

'Were you among the men who shot at me in Brannigan last night?' he hissed.

'No. That was Clancy.'

'Clancy Jarrett?'

'Yes.'

'How many of you are waiting for us?'

Dewey paused.

'Don't lie.' To add emphasis to his words, Al pressed the gun into him again.

'Five,' said Dewey.'

'Including you?'

'Yes.'

At that moment they both became aware of movement among the trees above them. Dewey's eyes shifted in that direction in the hope that the new arrivals would be his saviours, but, as Al suspected, Bart and the girl had grown impatient and were riding in search of him, heading towards the ambush. Al signalled for Dewey to move, pointing up the trail to where Bart and Kate would soon appear, keeping his gun tight against Dewey's spine so that he understood he needed to move quickly and stealthily and not in any way convey to his associates that he had deserted his post.

They intercepted Bart and Kate as they wended their way through the timber. As yet, they were not visible from the trail below but they had been less careful than Al in their descent and it was probable that the ambushers were aware of their proximity. Quickly, Al ordered them to dismount, told them of the ambush ahead and outlined his plan.

'His horse is tethered among those trees,' he told Bart. 'When I draw them away from the trail, you and the girl use it and keep going to Billings. Either I'll catch up or meet you there.'

Bart's protests were swept away by Al. 'One of us has to get the girl to Billings,' he insisted. While he spoke he tied Dewey's hands and ordered him to mount Kate's horse. After attaching the reins of that horse and Bart's to his own saddle horn, Al climbed on to his mount. 'Better keep your head down,' he told Dewey; then, drawing his handgun from its holster, he kicked his heels against his horse's flanks and began the descent.

Al set a course at right angles to the recognized downhill route. They emerged from the trees on to the valley trail, travelling fast, cutting straight across and heading for the river. Al yelled, a command for the horses to keep running but also a declaration of contempt for the ambushers, letting them know he was aware of their plot but that they weren't clever enough to catch him. It was also meant to add to their surprise for, although he needed them to see three horses racing for the river, he had to hope that they wouldn't realize that one of them carried one of their own men and that the saddle of the third was empty. To aid the deception, Al deliberately rode on the nearside, hoping his body, his yell and the two shots he fired up the trail would grab the attention of the ambushers.

Ahead, at the point where the trails converged and the

ambush had been set, a shout went up.

'That's them. They're making for the river.'

Shots sounded but they went well wide of the mark because Al heard neither the zing nor felt the movement of air caused by flying lead.

'Get the horses,' he heard someone order. He threw a glance in that direction to witness the commotion he'd caused. He could see four men, which tallied with what his prisoner had told him, who seemed rooted to the spot, completely surprised by his manoeuvre.

Then he was racing for the river, one arm outstretched, gripping Dewey's shirt, holding him in place lest he should attempt to part company with the horse and betray Al's deception. Dewey, however, was showing no interest in escape, he was, in fact, crouched low along the horse's neck, in full compliance with the instruction he'd been given. Al wondered if Dewey feared being hit, wondered if he credited his fellow ambushers with greater marksmanship than they had so far demonstrated. More gunshots sounded from behind, however, and they, too, proved untroublesome to the fleeing riders.

Unsure of the depth of water, Al nonetheless rode the horses into the river at full speed. But it was late summer and many weeks since the rivers and streams had been at full spate. The water in this course was no more than hock high as they covered the eight or nine strides to the far bank. Al cast another glance behind. Horses were being mounted and the pursuit was about to begin.

With the high ground behind them the territory at this side of the river was more fertile and lush with tall grass, bushes and, here and there, stands of cottonwoods and willows. Although the ground ahead lacked the dramatic ruggedness of the hills at their back, indeed as they raced forward it seemed almost flat, it was in fact a series of low rises and unexpected hollows into which, to the confusion of anyone watching or trailing, a rider could vanish. Al took advantage of those depressions, trying hard to extend the lead over the four men behind. At one point, looking back, he saw them on a rise, all four, and it gave him a surge of satisfaction to know that he'd drawn them across the river, allowing Bart and the girl to ride safely on towards Billings.

But now he had to figure out a way to save himself and elude his hunters. Not only that: he also had to decide what to do with his prisoner. To his surprise, the man had neither attempted to delay their flight nor escape. From time to time he too had cast backward glances but any sight of their pursuers seemed to be as much of a spur to him as it was to Al, as though he was just as determined to stay ahead of them. It was a turn of events that Al couldn't understand, but for the moment it wasn't the most important thing he had to worry about.

The horses were beginning to blow when an opportunity for respite and possible escape presented itself. They had breasted a long rise and below them lay a long, wide valley. Doubtless a river ran through it but Al could see no sign of it because the whole valley was thickly wooded. Once among those trees there would be no indication of which direction they had taken or on which side of the river they were hiding. Clancy could only continue the hunt by splitting his force and, in Al's experience, people like Clancy Jarrett needed to be certain of their superiority before tackling an opponent.

Al led the way among the trees, dismounted and

ordered Dewey out of the saddle. 'Stay quiet,' he told him.

'Never thought of doing otherwise,' responded Dewey.

They were in deep cover when Jarrett and his three followers rode slowly into the forest, looking left and right, hoping to pick up a sound or a sign that would indicate where the quarry had gone. One of them spoke but the words didn't carry and it didn't bring the quartet to a standstill. Al and Dewey watched as they passed by.

Silently they waited, Al keeping his gun pointed at Dewey, threatening to use it but knowing that if he did his hunters would be on to him in an instant. They waited several minutes until the sound of moving horses had gone. Then Al prepared to mount, but when Dewey reached for a saddle horn to do likewise, Al stopped him. 'You can wait here,' he said. 'They'll find you when they return.'

'I don't want Clancy to find me,' Dewey told him. 'He'll kill me for letting you get the best of me.' When Al seemed unimpressed with Dewey's declaration, giving him a look thick with disbelief, Dewey added, 'It's true. You don't know him. He's crazy. I've seen him shoot people who've failed him.'

'You should keep better company.'

'That's what I told Hank. We're not part of this. We just happened to be playing cards with him when Tulsa told him the girl was going to give evidence against him and that she had Jake Devane's money. Clancy seems to think the money belongs to him. That's what he really wants. After he killed the sheriff he ordered us to round up his horses when they were scattered. Honest, mister, Hank and me have no grudge against you. We don't even plan to stay in Brannigan. We're heading south.'

91

'You should have done it sooner.' Al was thinking that the fellow had been prepared to shoot him from ambush whether or not it was what he wanted to do, and, despite the man's obvious fear he still wasn't sure he could trust him. With a swift, unexpected movement, he cracked the man's skull with his pistol and left him unconscious on the ground.

Cautiously retracing his trail, he reached the edge of the forest. There he paused, senses alert in case Clancy Jarrett and his men had anticipated that he would circle back. When finally satisfied that there was no one else around, and with the spent horses in tow, he broke from cover and made a dash for the ridge. With luck, he figured, he'd catch up to Bart within an hour. Then the bullet struck, hitting the rear of his saddle and scaring his horse so that it reared with a frightened, hurt squeal. Al slipped off its back, hitting the ground with a painful, jarring thud.

Automatically he reached for his now holstered pistol but a voice warned against it.

'The oldest trick in the book, old man,' shouted Tulsa Jones who, despite Clancy Jarrett's derision at the suggestion, had doubled back, expecting such a ruse. 'Where are the others?'

'Gone,' Al told him. 'Well on the way to Billings. Gone to give evidence about the murder of our partner.'

For a moment Tulsa sat, digesting the information, confused by the presence of three horses and only one man. 'Well, you won't be joining them,' he said, and raised his rifle, an action to emphasize the end of the conversation.

A shot rang out but it came from behind Al. Tulsa threw his hands in the air and tumbled over the backside of his horse. He landed face down on the ground and remained still. Al turned to see Bart riding towards him.

'What are you doing here?'

'We agreed. We do this thing together.'

'The girl?'

'She's safe. Come on. Let's ride. Wherever the others are, they'll have heard the shots.'

They rode back to the river with many a backward glance but without any sign of pursuit. The day had darkened until it almost seemed like night, but it was only the storm clouds blocking out the sun. They found Kate safe in the rocky niche in which Bart had left her. Immediately she climbed on to a spare horse and they continued their journey to Billings. But they had only made half a mile when the storm broke.

CHAPTER SEVEN

Sleep had come easily to Hec Masters. Despite the out-burst of violence that had marked his departure from Lariat, the life of a United States marshal in the territory west of the Missouri was such that gunplay was common-place and death an accepted outcome. Hec Masters didn't go looking for such confrontations, but experience had taught him that, in a kill-or-be-killed situation, there was nothing to be gained by worrying about the outcome. He had done what he believed to be right to maintain the law, his conscience was untroubled by the death of a would-be assassin.

Many lawmen, he knew, would have been satisfied with nothing less than the death of all four men involved in the plot, or at least their capture and imprisonment, but Hec's decision, although arrived at swiftly, had been tempered by two considerations. First, the meeting with Cyrus Tobin and his boys had been one of chance and Hec hoped that the casualties they had suffered were sufficient to discour-age an ensuing vendetta.

More important, he was on his way to Brannigan to investigate a series of stagecoach robberies and outrages.

His intention was to conduct a covert investigation before revealing to anyone that he was a law officer, but news of his status would spread through the town like wildfire if he turned up with prisoners in tow.

He awoke with the sun and was in the saddle heading west before the morning chill had been chased away. A breeze came from the north, innocent at first but, as the hours passed, the gusts gained strength, bearing the suggestion of a storm. Distant dark clouds added to Hec's consternation. For a brief moment the idea of racing the storm to Brannigan passed through his mind, but he wasn't sure how far ahead the township lay or how fast the storm was travelling towards him. There was no profit in exhausting his horse if he was still in open country when the rain came. The only thing he was sure of was that a US marshal's badge gave him no immunity from the weather so his best course of action was to keep his eyes open for some form of shelter if the storm continued to head in his direction.

It was beyond noon when he crossed trails with a cavalry patrol. A grizzled sergeant told him he was unlikely to reach Brannigan that night as the storm would be upon them within an hour. He prophesied that it would be a rip-snorter and advised Hec to find shelter in the high ground.

A gust of wind whipped up Hec's horse's mane and tugged stubbornly at his coat. He clamped a hand to his hat and started his mount towards the high ground. Up high, gusts of wind brought the first drops of rain and the light of day receded to a dismal grey which extracted all grandeur from the natural panorama beyond. Hec rode carefully, keeping his horse on a short rein in case it should be spooked by a sudden roll of thunder or a lightning flash. He kept a lookout for a suitable spot which would provide shelter for himself and his horse, somewhere in which they might settle for several hours. A cleft which was just wide enough to accommodate them would have given adequate protection against the wind, but offered little shelter from above. He had an oilskin cape tied behind his saddle but it would be scant protection.

He pushed on, looking for an outcrop under which he could shelter or, better yet, a cave in which he and the horse could remain dry and where, with luck, he would be able to build a small fire to brew a pot of coffee.

His need to find a suitable place of shelter was fully occupying his thoughts when the bullet hit him. It ripped through his lower abdomen, just above his right hip, twisting him, wrenching from him a yell of pain and causing him to yank the reins with such violence that his startled horse reared. The rifle's report still resounded among the rocks as Hec fell, his back and head thudding against the rock floor, sending a fresh wave of pain through his body. At that moment of impact, as colours flashed behind closed eyes and his body was consumed by pain, he was no longer sure that he had any grip on consciousness.

He groaned, but beyond his pain a voice called, reaching through the agony and demanding his attention.

'Two of my boys, Masters. Two of my boys dead! Did you think I would let you ride away without payment? You are a dead man, Marshal Masters. A dead man.'

From the moment he hit the road, a similar thought had occupied Hec's mind. Never before had he known such pain, nor had he ever experienced such a sensation as that which currently overwhelmed him, the sensation that his life was draining away. His right hand, having found the wound in his side, was now smothered in his own blood and his vision was so blurred that he could barely discern the rocks that were strewn at the side of the trail. But Cyrus Tobin's taunt, for despite the agony that permeated his body and mind he knew the identity of his attacker, made him react like a man falling down a mountain reacts to his hand grasping a tough root, it gave him something to hold on to, something on which to focus his attention and use as base from which to climb back to the top.

I'm not dead yet, he told himself. I'm not dead yet but if I'm going then you're going with me.

Somewhere through the haze in his mind, Hec could hear Cyrus's voice. It wasn't loud as it had been when crowing over the felled marshal, but it was giving orders to Harv and Gus, urging them forward, he presumed, to finish off the job. Hec knew he had to move. If he remained on the trail he had no chance. But his judgement was so hindered that he couldn't tell how long he had been on the ground, or even how long it had taken him to decide that he had to move; if thinking was slow then movement, with its accompanying pain, was ten times worse.

Carefully, he raised his head, knowing that such a movement could be his last. Cyrus must know that he'd been hit and that if he wasn't already dead then he had to be hurt real bad. If he saw any movement, Hec suspected he would put another bullet in him without hesitation. What he saw, however, was that his horse had stopped only yards from where he lay and, he suspected, it currently formed a barrier between the Tobins and himself, obscuring their view. That was the reason why Cyrus was urging Harv and Gus to close in.

Praying that the horse didn't move, he moved his right hand slowly down from the hole in his side to the gun in his holster, wiping his hand along the rough material of his trousers in an attempt to clear away the blood with which it was covered. His hand had settled on the butt of the pistol when, under the horse's belly he saw the long legs of an approaching man. It wasn't until the man came around the horse's hindquarters that Hec saw the bandage round his head and knew that it was Harv.

Harv proved to be the wrong person to make the initial check on Hec Masters. Hec neither knew nor cared if Harv's lack of caution was due to the blow to the head he'd taken the previous night or simply a belief that the marshal was already dead, but he came clumsily down to the road and emerged from behind the horse, carrying his rifle across his body, the barrel pointing past his left shoulder. The look of surprise on his face when he saw Hec's pistol pointed square at his heart was the last expression he showed. Hec pulled the trigger instantly, the impact of the bullet throwing Harv on to his back, one leg bent at the knee, his rifle still gripped firmly in both hands. Cyrus Tobin yelled his name but his youngest son neither heard nor responded.

Even as he pulled the trigger, Hec Masters knew he couldn't remain where he lay. His bullet, which zipped behind his horse, close to its hindquarters, caused it to shy away a few steps, leaving Hec exposed to his enemies. With great will power, knowing he was committing himself to greater pain and not knowing if his system could endure it, he pushed himself into a rolling motion, leaving the trail and on to the downward slope beyond. If he lost consciousness he knew they would kill him wherever they found him.

The pain was indeed intense and the slope was steeper than he expected, which resulted in him rolling longer and further from the trail above. He hung on to consciousness, indeed, despite the moans that were forced from him as he descended, his desire for life seemed to have awakened a resolution that somehow dulled his physical discomfort. Snake like, but with the grace of a wounded boar, he sought the refuge of a chokeberry bush, burrowing in low, hoping his hiding place beneath the scratchy, spindly branches would give him enough time to take aim against his would-be killers before they spotted him.

He looked back up the slope. There was a clear path marking his descent. Here and there it was stained with his blood. He inspected his wound. It still bled. He wondered how much he'd lost, how much more he could afford to lose. He grabbed a handful of grass and pressed against the hole. He wasn't sure if it would do any good but figured it was better than doing nothing. He wondered if his dulled physical discomfort was attributable to his loss of blood, but if it was, it was a benefit which couldn't last much longer for his head felt empty; his thoughts seemed to be floating, barely graspable, but his limbs were heavy, a growing weakness for which blood loss was definitely responsible.

Above him, on the road he heard a shout, Gus confirming that Harv was dead. Now there were only two left, but Hec knew that Cyrus and Gus's approach would be more purposeful, more planned, determined to achieve revenge. When they came, Hec guessed, they would approach from two sides, circling wide, using whatever cover was available until they were close enough to finish him off. He surveyed the ground between himself and the trail above. There were plenty of bushes and trees and boulders available to provide cover for the Tobins. In his woozy state it would be difficult to keep track of one man's descent; two, in opposite directions, would be almost impossible. With difficulty, he opened the gate of his revolver, pulled out the used casing and replaced it with a cartridge from his belt. Six shots. In normal circumstances he'd back himself to take any two men with six shots, but as he closed the weapon and thumbed back the hammer he knew that these might be the last six bullets he fired.

Hec shuffled, tried to burrow lower to give himself more protection, more time before discovery. A long, straggling branch of the bush caught on his shirt, clinging to the rough material, eating into the period available to Hec to prepare for the coming attack. When at last he was free he noticed the elasticity of the branch, noted how it jumped, whiplike, back to its original position. Hec wondered if he could utilize this property of the bush to his advantage. Cyrus and Gus hadn't yet begun their advance although their voices carried to him from above.

He gripped the end of the springy branch, pulled its tip down to the ground so that it formed a tight bow that would be strong enough to fling a small object into the air. Hec chose his badge, slotting the top end of the tendril-like branch through the metalwork letters which declared him a US marshal.

Lying flat on the ground, his cocked pistol in his right hand and the drawn-back branch in his left hand, Hec awaited the oncoming Tobins. His assessment that they would work a pincer movement had been correct, but first they had peppered the area with gunshot, trying to flush out their prey to make the hunt easier. Several shots had hit the bush beneath which Hec lay, but they had all been too high. He had remained still while leaves and splinters fell all around.

His enemies were beginning to move when he took his first look in their direction. Gus was off to his left, heading for a high boulder in a crouching run. Cyrus, more ponderous, was also seeking the protection of some rocks. A fit Hec Masters would have taken advantage of the older man's slowness, would have shot him before he reached the safety of the rocks, but in his current situation he was incapable of acting quickly and any unnecessary movement would only advertise his position to his enemies.

Hec concentrated on Gus for two reasons. Gus was quicker than his father, was probably the one who would close in on him first. Also, if the badge was to be used as a decoy, it would fly off to Hec's left, in the direction from which Gus was approaching. The younger Tobin had left the security of the boulder and had moved lower down the slope seeking sanctuary behind a tree. Hec moved as little and as cautiously as possible, not wanting to draw attention to the bush but needing to sneak glances both ways if he hoped to pinpoint the location of both men. A prolonged gust of wind swept across the hillside, disturbing the leaves sufficiently to disguise any disturbance of the bush attributable to himself. Under such cover he was able to rise to his knees.

He peered through the dismal light, hoping to catch a glimpse of Cyrus Tobin, but without success. When he turned his attention to Gus he found the younger man had, like himself, taken refuge behind a bush which was less than twenty yards distant. Hec couldn't allow him to get any closer.

Another gust of wind blew, preventing Hec from releasing the tautly sprung branch. He wasn't sure what effect his improvised distraction would have on Gus, he wasn't even sure that it was strong enough to throw the badge beyond the bush, but apart from his pistol, which he gripped tightly in his bloody right hand, he had no other help. He checked on Gus again who seemed to be sending some sort of signal to his father. When Hec judged he was going to move forward again he released the branch. Silently, it whipped forward in a tight arc and at its zenith it launched the badge with greater velocity than Hec had suspected. Momentarily it flew, then landed silently on the grass.

Gus caught the movement out of the corner of his eye, swivelling and firing in one fluid, well-practised movement. But the shot flew off into empty space and Gus, bemused by the fact that there was nothing to see, took a step forward to investigate further. Marshal Hec Masters, though sorely wounded, needed no other opportunity. This was what he had planned and at such a distance he couldn't miss. He fired twice, both shots hitting Gus in the chest; he collapsed to his knees, then pitched full length on his face.

Hec had no opportunity to celebrate his victory. A shout from his right announced that Cyrus was closer than he'd expected and, after witnessing Gus's death, was advancing in a fury. He was yelling curses at Hec and firing his weapon, emptying it with speed if not great accuracy.

One of the bullets shattered Hec's left hand but the others missed him completely. Hec was unable to do anything quickly. His first shot hit Cyrus's left hip and he crumpled to the ground. Aiming carefully, Hec's second shot hit the old man in the head and he too, like his son, lay dead, face down on the ground.

Hec would never know how long it took him to reach the trail and his horse. It was a while before he moved, anchored to the spot by a combination of weakness and release from tension. Whether or not he passed out during the time he remained under the bush was something of which he had no clear recollection, but when, eventually, the proximity of the bodies of the Tobin gang impressed itself on his mind, he began to move. He was determined not to die in their company.

His progress up to the trail was slow, undertaken on hands and knees, but it was encouraged by two discoveries. First, although his shirt was caked in his own blood, the rate at which he was losing it seemed to have subsided. He was weak but still capable of thought and action. Therefore, he concluded, he hadn't yet lost sufficient to make the wound fatal.

The second discovery did nothing to heal his wound but it lifted his spirit in a way that nothing else could. His haphazard route took him beyond Gus's body and his hand fell on it, almost as though he had been guided there by some supernatural force. In the sunless day there was no glint from the dull metal, but finding his badge in the grass was as rewarding to him as gold nuggets in a stream bed. He pinned it to his jacket, gratified to know that whoever found his body would know that he had been a United States marshal.

His horse had remained at its station, the nervousness that had caused it to throw Hec from its back long forgotten. It waited while the marshal approached, turned its head from time to time to mark his progress but didn't make any move to shorten the distance between them. Hec was satisfied that it didn't move away from him and that it stood still while he pulled himself up by the stirrup leathers. Somehow he climbed into the saddle, pressed his heels to his steed's flanks, then fell forward on its neck as it responded to the order. Then the storm broke.

CHAPTER EIGHT

The rain fell with such sudden, cold force that the riders were instantly drenched and breathless, but within moments they were aware of every large, individual drop that struck and burst against them. Those that hit a face were almost painful, especially when driven to their target by a wind which had become almost constant. Rainwater saturated their clothing and ran down their faces before they could equip themselves with any form of protection. The first impact drove a squeal from Kate as the breath was forced from her body. She gasped as she tried to refill her lungs, only to discover that that was not a simple matter. The cold shock made her body convulse and shiver at the same time. Open-mouthed and wide-eyed she turned a frightened face to Bart.

Like all drovers, Bart and Al knew all about the force of a storm in open country and had set out on the cattle drive duly prepared. Each man carried a heavy-duty oilskin cape rolled behind his saddle and, at the onset of rain, the two cowboys had reined in their mounts and reached for them. Bart shouted to the girl to use Walt's. Because of the noise of the storm and her general disorientation from breathlessness she had difficulty understanding him. Setting aside his own needs Al drew his mount close to hers and undid the strings that tied the roll to her saddle. He shook out the cape and helped her into it.

By the time all but her lower legs were covered, her breathing had settled once more into its natural rhythm and Bart attended to his own protection. For the moment there was little more he could do. Beneath the cape the girl was thoroughly soaked, but so were he and Al and the rain was likely to continue for hours. Their best plan was to find some form of shelter, preferably away from the recognized trail in case Clancy Jarrett was determined to continue the pursuit. He turned to Al, such a suggestion close to his lips, but his partner was studying the land behind them. They were there, four distant riders following in the tracks they'd made from the far river.

'Do you think they've seen us?' Bart shouted above the storm.

'Hard to say. But we can't stay here.'

Bart nodded. 'Can't go on too much further, either.' He pointed at the water pools already forming on the rocky surface of the trail. 'Won't be safe to run the horses soon. Don't want them slipping.'

'They are already tired,' Al said. 'But so are theirs.'

'Let's put some more ground between us, but we need to find shelter soon.'

They rode on, picking a steady pace, the thought in Bart's mind that the darkness of the day and the black capes might be camouflage enough to escape the notice of their enemies. He threw a look behind. What he saw didn't please him. The group behind was closer, a grim indicator that they had been seen.

Half an hour later the horses, exhausted by the additional battle with the elements, were blowing hard. Steam rose from them as they circled. Al pointed off to his left.

'Up there,' he insisted. 'Let's get off the trail. The ground here is too hard to leave tracks. If Jarrett and his men are still following they'll probably ride straight past.'

'All the way to Billings,' murmured Bart, meaning that once Jarrett and his men were ahead of them a showdown was inevitable at some point – and at a point of Clancy's choosing.

'Do you want to wait here and pick them off as they come down the trail?'

'That's what they would do to us,' Bart said, but he wasn't a gunman; the thought of bushwhacking any man didn't sit easy with him.

Al's expression indicated that he was of the same opinion. 'Come on then,' he said, putting his mount to the climb. 'Let's see if we can give them the slip and find some refuge.'

In single file they climbed. After a few steps they dismounted when Al espied a way up the hillside which had enough rocks and tree foliage to provide them with cover from the trail if Jarrett and his men rode by below. Kate was drained by the events of the last twenty-four hours and found the climb difficult. Al paused a few moments at each station along the way that hid them from sight of the trail below. Although anxious to reach as far up the hillside as possible before those following riders reached the spot where they'd left the trail, he was not unaware of Kate's physical distress. Like the horses, she needed respite from the power of the storm.

They'd reached a point which would take them round

to the far side of the hill but which still provided a good view of the trail below.

'You go on with Kate,' Bart told Al. 'I'll wait here. Watch what they do. I'll catch up shortly.'

'We stick together,' said Al.

'We are sticking together,' Bart told him, 'but she needs rest and there's nowhere here to shelter.'

Al threw a glance at Kate. 'If I hear shooting I'll be back.'

'No. If you hear shooting you've got to stay with the girl. Get her to Billings for Walt's sake.' When Al stared hard at him he added, 'I doubt if it will come to that. If they haven't already sought shelter themselves I doubt if they'll expect it of us.'

Unsatisfied yet unable to summon up an argument, Al turned away. He spoke to Kate who followed where he led, so weary was she that she barely comprehended that Bart had remained behind.

They climbed up and round the hill, but the change of direction gave them no respite from the fury of the weather. If anything, Al found himself working harder, bending forward, driving himself on into the full force of the wind as the rain lashed his face and struck against his cape with a sound like fleeing rats on a tar-cloth roof. He glanced back. Kate too was bent into the wind, holding down her hat with one hand, pulling the reins with the other.

They had struggled on in this fashion for fifteen minutes before Al saw the entrance to the cave. At first, because it was slightly above them and angled away from their direction of approach, he wasn't sure it was anything more than a slight recess in the rock face. However, any hope of shelter was worth investigating and when he saw the full opening and became aware that the space within was at least big enough to get them out of the rain, he gave Kate a big grin.

'Come on,' he said. 'If it's deep enough we may be able to get a fire started.'

From his vantage point on the hillside Bart watched the trail for ten minutes. Using an outcrop on the hillside for cover, he was certain that in the current conditions no one on the trail below would pick him out. He dropped the horse's reins, knowing that it wouldn't wander far away. In fact it stood quietly at his side, sorry for itself in the torrential rain but too weary to seek shelter. Bart, too, disliked the weather. The oilskin cape was effective now, but beneath it his soaked clothing still clung to his body. Rainwater fell in a constant stream from the side gunnels of his high-crown hat.

With attention focused on their own back trail, trying to see through the driving rain and the enveloping gloom for the chasing group, it came as a surprise to Bart when a rider approached from the opposite direction. The horse was moving slowly, not just unhappy in the rain as his own beast was, but drifting, unguided, lost in unfamiliar territory. The sight of the rider's slumped form brought Bart to his feet. The man was clearly in trouble, clinging to his mount's neck, allowing it to take him where it would.

Even though his own troubles were close at hand and deadly, it wasn't in Bart's nature to ignore someone in need. He cast another glance into the western darkness, then began to scramble down the hillside to the trail below. The horse was well-schooled and paused on the trail when it became aware of Bart, allowing him to approach and grip its bridle while he spoke softly to it. The man on the beast's back didn't move and despite the saturated condition of his clothing, the telltale blotches of blood still showed. Momentarily, Bart thought the man was dead, but when he lifted his head a low, life-confirming moan rolled in the rider's throat.

Bart cast another glance west. If Jarrett and his men were still in pursuit they were bound to be close at hand. He couldn't afford to dally here on the trail, but nor was he willing to leave the man unattended for there was no hope of succour for him from Clancy Jarrett. One glance at the hillside posed another problem for Bart. He didn't know how long horse and man had travelled in this fashion, but he figured it couldn't have been far; the man would surely have fallen if there had been any deviation from the level trail. Acting swiftly, he led the horse to the side of the trail and used the man's own rope to tie him to the saddle.

Then they began the climb. They hadn't gone a dozen strides before Bart heard the sound of his pursuers. Handicapped as they were by the weather conditions and weary animals, those approaching weren't travelling fast and Bart knew he had to find cover until they'd passed by. There was adequate foliage at this lower level, into which Bart steered the horse. When the band of four rode past without a glance in his direction, Bart was satisfied that, for a few hours at least, they were free of Clancy Jarrett.

When his pursuers disappeared, swallowed by the curtains of rain that swept across the trail, Bart commenced his uphill trek. With continuous checks on the safety of the wounded rider, it took several minutes to reach the point where his own horse still waited. He had no idea how far ahead Al and Kate were, nor if they had found a refuge. In worsening weather he climbed, the torrential downpour reducing Bart's visibility until he was no longer certain that he was following his friend's route. Suddenly, his horse gave out a shrill neigh. A familiar, answering whinny came from close at hand. Within moments he saw Al waving urgently from a depression in the hillside.

An hour after being pistol-whipped by Al Dunnin, Dewey Shillitoe was still suffering from the effects of the blow. The hard pace set by Clancy Jarrett wasn't helping his recovery but at least the pain meant that he was still alive and he was thankful for that. He wasn't blind to the fact that having been discovered in an attempted ambush, the cowboy had had every reason to kill him. He could only suppose that the long ride across the river to the far copse where they'd avoided the gang had smothered any immediate desire for revenge and the thought of a cold-blooded killing had become distasteful to him. Of course, there was also the fact that a gunshot would betray the cowboy's position and nothing that he or his beef-pushing friend had so far done had hinted that they were stupid. Nonetheless, Dewey was grateful to be alive.

The unknown cowboy wasn't the only one to whom he owed a debt. His own partner, Hank Pardoe, had come to his assistance when, semi-concussed, he'd staggered to the spot where he, Clancy and Sepp Minto were gathered around Tulsa's body. As Dewey had anticipated, because their quarry had escaped the trap, Clancy was in a murderous mood and in need of someone on whom he could vent his anger. The narrow-eyed, thin-lipped way he'd

111

studied Dewey's approach had left no one in any doubt that he'd found his target.

For an instant, it seemed as though Clancy would gun down Dewey in like manner to his killing of Ollie Dent after the failed stagecoach robbery, but Hank had prevented it or, at the very least, delayed it. He'd stepped forward, pointing back towards the river where they'd waited in ambush, giving voice to the fact that he had briefly seen their quarry before losing sight of them again in the undulations of the terrain. It was a lie. Hank had seen nothing, speaking up only to distract Clancy from his evil intent. His follow-up comment found its mark, too, a reference to their reduced number.

'Let's get after them,' Clancy had declared, reluctantly because it betrayed his need for a superior force, although the mean look he cast Dewey's way was a clear signal that he blamed him for the failed ambush.

Dewey muttered his thanks as Hank boosted his partner into Tulsa's empty saddle. 'We've got to get away,' he said.

'Sure,' agreed Hank, 'but not yet awhile. He'll be watching us like a hawk and he won't need much reason to kill us.'

So they'd set off in the wake of Clancy and Sepp who were making a hurried beeline in the direction Hank had indicated. Dewey was woozy and his eyesight unsure. His head pounded with every stride and his stomach tightened and jumped as though he would soon be spreading along the trail the hardtack and beans he'd eaten earlier that day. Soon he was adrift of his friend, too, but rode on as best he was able until the storm broke and he came upon all three on a ridge overlooking the river close to the point where the ambush had been set.

'That's them,' Hank said, managing to restrain his amazement that he had directed Clancy towards Kate and the cowboys.

'Let's go,' snarled Clancy, and he put his mount to the down slope, determined that this time there would be no escape. By the time they'd forded the river their quarry was out of sight and, in the worsening storm, their weary horses were proving reluctant to continue the chase. Although his followers were also reluctant to press on, Clancy's rough urging of the beast beneath him made it clear that he was not yet ready to submit to the elements. Covering himself with his long duster he yelled at the others, exhortations meant to convince them that those they were chasing would be just as reluctant to continue in these conditions and couldn't be far ahead. Spurring his mount again, he urged it on into the face of the storm.

Clancy, Sepp and Hank forged on for fifteen minutes, each of them drenched, rain lashing their faces until it was almost too painful to keep their eyes open, water finding a path beneath their collars, saturating their cotton under-garments and chilling the skin beneath. They rode with lowered heads, as if they were trying to shoulder their way through an advancing crowd, as if their own brute strength could overcome nature's force.

A dozen paces behind them, Dewey was desperate to stop, needing stillness to rescue him from the gut-churning pain in his head. He was almost breathless and his discomfort and reluctance to proceed were transmitted to the steed beneath him. It was snorting and steaming, moving forward with a rolling, uneven gait. For a moment it turned sideways to the storm, taking the full brunt of a wind gust, almost slipping to its knees, registering its alarm

113

by throwing its head high and emitting a startled whinny. Dewey cursed, hauled on the reins and brought the horse round in a full circle while it regained its balance and shook itself to shed the water trapped in its coat.

And that was when Dewey thought he caught sight of someone on the hillside, a rider, lunging forward as though clinging to his animal's neck as it tackled the incline. His own horse turned again and by the time he'd pulled it back into position, the rider had gone, leaving Dewey wondering if what he'd seen had been a mirage, a mixture of his own confusion and images distorted by the wind-scattered rain.

Eventually, he shrugged. Even if it had been one of the men they were pursuing he wasn't going to tell Clancy. Whatever Jarrett had against those people it wasn't his fight. The sooner and the further he and Hank got away from Clancy Jarrett the happier he would be.

A mile further along the trail Dewey caught up with the other three. The chill he experienced at that moment had nothing to do with the violence of the weather. For a moment he experienced the sensation of something tightening around his throat, as though a rough rope noose had rubbed against his neck. Each man had dismounted and now stood over a bloody body. Dewey couldn't recall hearing gunfire as he'd approached but the noise of the storm, he supposed, had disguised the sounds of discharge. It was Clancy who broke his moment of panic, asking the others if they recognized the men they were examining. No one did.

Dewey took a look at the bodies of Cyrus Tobin and his boys and shook his head along with everyone else when it came to identification.

'I'd say they've been dead less than an hour,' declared Clancy. 'They weren't killed by Kate and her friends.' Anxiously, he looked around the killing site, as though expecting the killer to be still close at hand.

'Tell you something else that Kate and her friends haven't done,' said Sepp Minto, rejoining the group after walking the trail towards Billings. 'They haven't passed this way.' Clancy eyed him, making it obvious that he needed Sepp to complete his report. 'The ground is a lot softer around here. No horses have passed here recently. I reckon those cowboys are someplace behind us. They must have taken shelter from the weather.'

'That's what we should do,' muttered Hank. 'The beasts are all in. We'll kill them if we ask any more of them and what good will it do us to be afoot?'

Clancy glared at him but he knew there was sense in Hank's words; it was just that he didn't like being forced to agree.

'OK,' he said, 'let's find some shelter. This rain can't continue much longer and when they hit the trail again we'll be ready for them.'

CHAPTER NINE

The cave Al had found exceeded his expectations. Once inside, rather than the hillside crevice he had originally taken it to be, he found it larger and shaped so that the deepest portion almost formed a separate chamber. Immediately, he'd gathered some of the wind-blown twigs that littered the floor and by the time they were reunited with Bart, a small fire was burning, providing both light and life-saving warmth.

While untying the man from his horse, Bart related his story. Between them, Al and Bart carried the wounded man through to where the fire burned.

Al examined the blood-soaked clothing and the bullet hole in the man's side. 'I'm not sure there's anything we can do for him.'

'Can't you dig out the bullet?'

'I don't think there's any lead in there. Holes back and front. I guess he was shot clean through. Trouble is we've got nothing we can use to clean the wound. We can rip up our spare shirts for padding but I think he's lost a lot of blood. I wonder who he is?'

Kate picked up the jacket Al had removed from the

injured man. 'Look,' she said, holding it up so that the others could see the badge over the pocket. 'He's a US marshal.'

The irony of the situation was not lost on any of the trio: they were seeking a lawman who could deliver justice for them, but the one they'd found was in a worse plight than they were themselves. They cleaned the marshal's wound and padded it to stem the flow of blood, but Al's low grunt when he'd completed his doctoring carried the suggestion that what he'd done might be too little, too late.

Clancy's prediction that the rain couldn't continue much longer couldn't have been more wrong. The torrential downpour continued throughout the night and barely eased until well past noon the next day. On a shelf above the trail they erected a crude shelter against the hillside, covering a framework of hastily harvested branches with their waxed long coats, the end-product being a totally inadequate refuge for men and horses, but one which Clancy refused to abandon. Despite the grumbles of the other three men, Clancy would not listen to any argument in favour of returning to Brannigan. No matter how uncomfortable their enforced sojourn, neither Kate nor her friends nor Jake Devane's money were going to make it to Billings. This site gave them a commanding view of the trail below. When the trio made their move they were bound to pass this point. Then Clancy would have them, and that moment couldn't come soon enough.

Al, Bart and Kate were well sheltered in the cave but during the night Hec Masters was gripped with fever.

117

However, any doubts that were harboured about his strength or determination to survive were dispelled the following day. His fever passed with the night and he slept soundly for another four hours, waking, eventually, with gradually remembered details of the gunfight with Cyrus Tobin and his boys and the wounds he'd received.

He couldn't work out how that event had led to him being in this place with these people and his first attempts to grapple with the problem inevitably led him back to sleep. At his next awakening he clung on to consciousness long enough to hear how Bart had found him. By all rights, Bart told him, with the wound he'd received, he should be dead, but he said it with a grin, showing some admiration for Hec's constitution.

By this time the wild wind had abated, had moved south, the tempest was almost over. Food was now the main concern. The invalid was hungry and nourishment was essential for his recovery. Bart remarked to his older companion that the hills must be full of game but they both knew that a gunshot could signal their location to Clancy and his men.

However, during the last days of the Civil War, when Al and his Confederate comrades had faced starvation, they had devised a means of catching rabbits with a grass noose. It hadn't just been fear of discovery by Union soldiers that had prompted this manner of hunting, but the lack of ammunition for their guns. Al was confident that he could still remember how it was done, so, when the rain stopped, he and Bart left the cave to try their luck. Bart was to act as lookout while Al hunted, there was no point catching a rabbit only to be surprised by one of Clancy's crew.

118

It was when Bart voiced the opinion that Jarrett and his men had probably returned to Brannigan that Al recalled the conversation with the man he'd pistol-whipped across the river. He told Bart of Clancy's belief that the girl had some money that was rightly his and that that was the reason for the pursuit. They agreed to question Kate about it when they returned to the cave.

Their hunt was successful. They returned with two rabbits. However, for Kate, meat for a meal was only the second best news of the day. While Bart and Al had been hunting, she and Hec had exchanged stories.

Kate's tale about the killing of Sheriff Oates, the discovery that her sister and Jake Devane had been killed and the subsequent pursuit by Clancy Jarrett, brought a surprising response from the US marshal.

'Are you Kate Jeavons?' he'd asked, and receiving an affirmative answer proceeded to pass on some information that both surprised and delighted her. Alice was alive. The story he related was that Jake Devane had, indeed, attempted to rescue Alice and had almost succeeded, but their flight had been ended along the trail to Billings. Jake had been killed, a deed witnessed by Alice, who had evaded death by leaping from her horse when it stumbled over the hillside trail.

Stunned and frightened, Alice had lain unobserved below the lip of the mountain road and had watched as Clancy shot Jake dead. A farmer had found her afoot next day and brought her to Billings. Her injuries were slight, Hec told Kate, but it was her testimony that had instigated his journey to Brannigan with orders to arrest Clancy Jarrett.

Later that night, as they feasted on the rabbit meat, Hec

Masters elaborated on Alice's attestation against Clancy Jarrett, citing evidence she had that included terrorization of Brannigan, highway robbery as well the murder of Jake Devane. To these, Bart added the killing of Walt Dickers and Sheriff Oates, and the attempted ambush in which he'd planned to kill himself, Al and Kate.

'But you can't continue with your mission,' Al said. 'You're not likely to get any help from the citizens of Brannigan.'

At that point, Bart spoke of the money that Kate was reported to be carrying.

Kate rejected the suggestion. 'The only money I have is what Jake gave me to hold for him. It was to be the means for me, him and Alice to start anew in Cheyenne. It has nothing to do with Clancy Jarrett.'

Al told her what Dewey Shillitoe had divulged, that Jake had been involved in the stagecoach hold-ups. 'What did Jake do in Brannigan?'

'He worked for the silver mine. In the company office.'

'It was the mining company's payrolls that were stolen.' Hec Masters's voice was low and sombre, clearly implying that Jake Devane had been involved in robbery.

Kate laughed at the suggestion. The only risks Jake Devane was likely to take were those that involved the cards in his hand. Then she remembered that he had attempted to rescue her sister, an act she would never have believed possible. Perhaps she hadn't know the man as well as she thought. When she'd found the money she'd assumed he'd won it at the high-stake tables in Missoula. That made it honest money to her, and she wasn't going to let it slip away from her and Alice now.

Meanwhile, Al advised Hec against proceeding to

Brannigan, urging him to return with them to Billings.

'Seems sensible,' said Bart, 'providing we can avoid Jarrett. You were lucky to survive the bushwhack set up by those other killers. You'll live but I reckon your body needs some time to mend. If we stay here undetected for another couple of days he'll probably think he's lost us.'

Al drew Bart aside. 'When are we going to get back to the herd? Mr Jefford will be hopping like a green-horned toad.'

'He'll get over it when he hears the full story. Our lives are on the line here, Al. We can only do our best.'

So it was agreed that they would remain hidden until Hec was stronger for travel. By that time they hoped that Clancy Jarrett would have given up the hunt for them, but they knew that the killer could be waiting in ambush every step of the way to Billings.

Even when the rain stopped, the incessant drip of rain-drops from the trees above could still be heard in the make-shift camp that housed Clancy and his crew. An atmosphere of fear and danger hung around the men; no one was willing to look into anyone else's eyes, least of all Clancy's, which were now wild with distrust. In turn during their miserable vigil, the others had complained and argued against the continuation of the hunt until Clancy, in wild-eyed fury, had proclaimed that he wasn't going to be outwitted by a dance-hall harlot or trail-dusty cowboys. They weren't going to reach Billings and nor was Jake Devane's money. That was rightly his and he would kill anyone who prevented him from getting his hands on it. He'd glared at each of them in turn, leaving no room for doubt that he would back up the threat.

Dewey Shillitoe suspected that the only reason Clancy didn't open fire on them there and then was so that he didn't announce his presence to Kate and her friends. So, when the rain ceased and Clancy ordered each of them to search an area from the high ground to the river, they were all eager to do his bidding.

Sepp Minto had patrolled the high ground, looking for evidence that their quarry was still in the vicinity between their camp and the place where they'd attempted to ambush them the previous day. On different levels, Dewey and Hank had done likewise; Dewey sticking close to the recognized trail while Hank rode further south to the river and searched for signs that the trio they were chasing had crossed it once more. Clancy had covered the road ahead, had ridden some miles towards Billings without finding any fresh hoofprints in the muddy sections of the trail.

It was during Sepp's slow return to camp that he saw Bart and Al. It had been only a fleeting, distant sighting but he knew he had not been mistaken. The men had been wending their way downhill, one of them carrying dead rabbits. Sepp had dismounted, led his horse behind a jagged outcrop from where he hoped to get a clear shot at them, but just as suddenly as he'd seen them, they'd disappeared. On foot he'd gone in search of them, hoping to find some indication of the route to their hideaway.

Darkness was descending when he gave up the search, having found nothing but a muddy skid mark where a foot had slipped on the hard, wet surface. He never knew how close he'd been to the band of four, nor that the sound from a cave below was not the warning growl of some wild animal alerted by his nearness but the snort of a bored horse, the noise distorted by the hollow cavern in which it was stabled. However, as he'd made his way back to his own horse he'd vowed to return. In the morning, when they set out hunting again, he would be waiting.

It was only as he was riding back to camp that he realized he had no intention of reporting his discovery to Clancy. He recalled the look on Clancy's face earlier that day and the threat he'd made. During the past few days he'd seen Clancy on the edge of insanity. He remembered the callous treatment of Ollie Dent, the young kid in the Prairie Rose, and of Sheriff Oates. Clancy had gunned them down with the same amount of care he'd have shown for a rabid dog, and Sepp knew that if he hung around much longer the same fate would befall him. The money the girl had was as much his as it was Clancy's, so he would take it and ride off West to someplace where Clancy would never find him.

Dewey Shillitoe too, was afraid of Clancy Jarrett, and was determined to leave his company at the first opportunity. All day he had wanted to talk with Hank Pardoe, had wanted to persuade him to quit this manhunt. It wasn't their argument, he wanted to tell Hank, although they were probably implicated in the killing of the Brannigan sheriff even though they had been nothing more than witnesses, like every other man who had been outside the Red Garter that night.

But the opportunity to talk with his partner had never arisen. They had been confined to the rough shelter most of the day, had been shoulder to shoulder with Clancy Jarrett, which had curtailed free speech. Later, when they'd ridden out to search for the girl and her friends, Hank had swiftly put his mount to a gallop, getting it to stretch out after the cramped conditions in which the horses had been hitched. He'd crossed the trail towards the river before Dewey had had any chance to speak to him. However, Dewey resolved to speak to him at first light. They would leave Clancy Jarrett to his own fate.

CHAPTER TEN

Some hours earlier, shortly before noon, Virgil Jefford had reached Brannigan. The trail boss was no longer able to quell the disquiet that had grown in him throughout the previous day. Al, Bart and young Walt Dickers should have returned long before nightfall. There were other men on the payroll who, released temporarily from the dust and rigours of a trail drive, might have succumbed to the whiskey and painted women available in the saloons and bawdy-houses of a frontier town, but not those three.

Al and Bart had been with him for several years. He knew their character, knew them to be sensible men, trusted them to attach the same level of importance to the completion of their task as he would himself. In addition, they understood the needs of trailing cattle over a long distance. Not only were the provisions they'd been sent to collect essential, but their absence demanded more of the remaining crew. They were the sort of men who would return to their duties as drovers as soon as possible.

As for young Walt, he was still so wet behind the ears that he wouldn't refill his cup from the campfire coffee pot without first seeking permission from the cook. He wouldn't cause trouble in Brannigan, wouldn't breathe without checking first with Al or Bart.

Curly Timms and he had left the herd early, had thrown their saddles over a pair of big striding geldings when the sun had been nothing more than a yellow-pink stain on the eastern horizon. Virgil had left Pete Wheeler, the ramrod, in charge until his return, giving the order to move slowly and keep the herd tight. It wouldn't do to have the cattle spread across the open grassland. With only five men remaining to drive them onwards they couldn't afford to send anyone after strays.

There had been the expected cold edge to the morning, the sky had been high and clear, a portent of another day of heat and dust, but the further north Virgil and Curly rode the darker the eastern sky had become and the tumult of a distant storm became more evident. Virgil hoped it wasn't on a course that would intercept the cattle. Pete Wheeler and the boys had their hands full already; a prairie storm panicking the beasts was the last thing they needed. Virgil kept an eye on the storm's progress but they reached Brannigan before the rain fell. The clouds were low, black and heavy and the cowmen's sympathies were with anyone caught in that downpour.

Virgil and Curly were forced to rein in their horses at the edge of town to give precedence to a funeral cortège heading to the high ground to the north of Brannigan. It was a long procession: the hearse, an inelegant cart of black painted boards pulled by two black horses, was already part of the way up the hill, but such was the number of mourners that half the stream of those walking in its wake had still to pass before the cowmen could complete their journey into town.

'Must have been a popular man,' Curly remarked as they made a beeline for the sheriff's office. To Virgil's thinking, the sheriff was the right person to speak to first. The lawman would be acquainted with any incident involving his men. But they were met by a locked door.

Virgil nodded his head in the direction of the Prairie Rose. 'Let's try over there,' he said. It seemed logical to him that if Al, Bart and Walt had got this far they would have needed to wash the dust of the trail from their throats. Curly, his tongue passing briefly across his lips, wasn't going to look for an argument against a visit to the saloon.

Three girls were gathered at the far end of the long bar. Apart from dresses of similar design, which displayed bare chests and black-stocking-clad legs, they seemed to have little in common with each other. They differed in age, height, colouring and style. One smoked a long, brown cheroot, occasionally spitting small shreds of tobacco from her lips. Another was talking, but it was doubtful if either of the other two was listening to her. When Virgil pushed his way through the batwings their indolence slid from them like it does from out-posted sentries surprised by a three-star general. They preened, smiled, moved their bodies with what they hoped was beguilement. Virgil's cold surveillance of the near-empty room finally rested on them and immediately they knew that the blankness of his hard-eyed stare killed any hope of business.

'I'm looking for three of my riders,' stated Virgil. He spoke to the barman but his voice rang in every corner of the hollow shell of a saloon. 'They should have reached here two days ago,' he continued. 'Al Dunnin. Bart Sween. Walt Dickers.' He paused between each name so that individually they filled the room for a moment. No one spoke.

'Do those names mean anything to you?' He moved his gaze from one face to the next. 'Do you know their current whereabouts?'

Still no one answered, but the silence was uncomfortable, as if there were words to be said but no one present had the authority to speak them.

'Don't know them,' the barman eventually answered. Once again, Virgil cast a look around the room. He didn't believe the barman but it was too soon to threaten violence. He'd come to find his boys and he was prepared to ask his questions of everyone in town until someone provided the answers. Abruptly he turned and with Curly hot on his heels, went outside to the street.

'Find a livery stable,' he told Curly. 'Have the horses tended to. I'm going to that storehouse.' He pointed at the opposite building which had Harper's Mercantile painted in huge red letters high on the wooden frontage. 'That's where they would have gone for the supplies.'

'You Harper?' His abrupt question was directed at a slim young man filling shelves at the rear of the store. The gruff sound of Virgil Jefford's voice startled the busy clerk.

'No sir. Mr Harper is up at the funeral. Can I help?'

'If you can tell me the whereabouts of my drovers. They should have arrived here two days ago needing a bundle of supplies to get us through to Cheyenne. I expect this would be the place they'd come for them.'

'Couldn't rightly say,' the young man told him. 'I don't work here every day. Just filling in this morning while Mr Harper's at the funeral and the town meeting after that.'

A sound rumbled in Virgil Jefford's throat, like a grizzly that had picked up a strange scent, but Virgil wasn't a man who easily lost his temper. He knew the fellow wasn't being deliberately evasive, and grumbling at his lack of knowledge wouldn't get him anywhere, but Virgil's voice reflected his frustration when he declared, 'I'll be back later.'

The young man watched him leave, saw him pause on the boardwalk, then saw him make his way up the street with the rolling gait of someone who spends a lot of time in the saddle. It was then that he thought of the sacks and packs that Mr Harper had set aside for collection. Perhaps they were for the drovers the man was seeking. The urge to call out to the man lasted less than a moment. He'd said he would return. Mr Harper would deal with the matter when he came back.

Virgil looked up and down the almost deserted street, rueing the misfortune of an ill-timed arrival but resigning himself to the fact that his enquiries must be delayed for at least another half hour, until the townsfolk returned from the cemetery. Further along the street, in the direction Curly had gone with the horses, an eating-house caught Virgil's eye. If he had to wait for the town to return to normal activity he might as well use the time to fill his own needs. The place was empty and Virgil chose a window seat to enable him to intercept Curly when he was through at the stable.

The woman who brought him coffee was round-faced and round-figured. An unexpected customer brought a smile to her face and a desire to chatter that wasn't deterred by Virgil Jefford's stern and rough appearance.

'You're new to town?' she asked.

'Just arrived.'

'We're a quiet town,' she said, accompanying the words with a warm smile that diminished slightly when she added, 'usually.' The reason for the lack of customers and passers-by subdued her spirits.

Virgil looked through the window at the empty street and nodded an agreement.

'Do you intend to stay in Brannigan long?' asked the woman.

'No, ma'am.'

'Here on business?'

'You could say that. Three of my hands headed this way to collect supplies. They failed to get back to the herd. I'm here to find out what happened to them.'

'Three men?'

'Yes, ma'am. I mean to speak to your sheriff. I figure he's up at that funeral. Seems like most folk in town are.'

'Yes,' she said, softly, not sure what more she should say to the cattleman. She picked up a copy of *The Clarion* and placed it beside his cup, seemingly to provide him with something of interest but in reality to give her a reason to break off the conversation. It was only when she reached the doorway that led through to the kitchen that she remembered the story that occupied most of the front page. When she looked back she knew by the depth of his engrossment that he was reading about the interrupted stagecoach robbery.

Virgil raised his head, his eyes met hers. A low chuckle escaped his lips.

'Heroes,' he said. 'Made themselves heroes, have they?' The fact that the woman was no longer smiling seemed strange to him but a sudden rap on the window distracted him from wondering why. He waved an arm, signalling for Curly to join him inside.

'Two of our horses are already in the stable,' Curly

blurted out before he'd even crossed the room to the table where his boss sat. 'At least we know they reached town.'

Virgil's ever active mind registered that if only two of his horses were in the stable then three were unaccounted for, but so were his three men so it was logical to assume that horses and men were together in some other part of town. But for the moment their whereabouts was a secondary matter. His humour was tickled by the article he'd read in the newspaper.

'They sure did,' he told Curly. 'Read this. Chased off some highwaymen. Walt's a hero.' Virgil tried to get some mirth in his words but the expression on the eating-house woman's face somehow stifled it. 'What is it?' he asked her. 'Where are the boys?'

She fidgeted with the hem of her apron but couldn't tear her eyes away from the cattleman's face. 'The young one,' she said, hesitating before finishing her sentence, 'He's dead. Killed in a gunfight.'

The cold expression on Virgil's face frightened the woman. He looked down at the newspaper as though needing to reassure himself that the name that figured so frequently in its dramatic front-page story was indeed that of the boy who'd been part of his crew from the north country.

'Walt Dickers? Dead?'

Curly Timms was no less startled. 'A gunfight?' The two words were laden with astonishment and disbelief.

'Who did it?'

Virgil's voice was low and even but the woman divined it to be no less full of anger than if he'd overturned tables and thrown the coffee pot through the window. 'Clancy Jarrett,' she said, looking him in the eyes because, fearsome as he seemed at that moment, she knew that none of his angry power was directed at her.

'Does the sheriff have him locked up?'

The woman shook her head.

'Why not?' queried Virgil, but the words were merely a spoken thought. He expected no answer from the woman and continued to give voice to the workings of his mind. 'That boy never handled a gun in his life. That was murder, not a gunfight.' He turned to Curly. 'That sheriff has some questions to answer when he returns from the cemetery.'

'He won't be returning,' said the woman. Her words caught the attention of the cattlemen. 'It's Sheriff Oates who is being buried.' She paused. 'Clancy Jarrett killed him, too.'

'And where is Jarrett now?'

'He's gone. Left town.'

'With a posse after him?' It flashed through Virgil Jefford's mind that Bart and Al had ridden out with the posse to make sure that Walt's killer was brought to justice. Under those circumstances he could forgive their late return.

'No,' the woman said.

'What kind of town is this?' Curly wanted to know.

'A good town.' The woman's answer was defiant. 'Perhaps something bad has happened here but it doesn't make Brannigan an evil place.'

'Yet a young boy and your sheriff are killed and no one does anything about it?' Virgil was finding it hard to contain his anger.

'The men in this town aren't gunfighters,' the woman declared. 'But a town meeting is planned to decide what to do.'

People were passing the window, mourners returning from the funeral. Virgil recalled the young man in the mercantile store telling him he was deputizing for Mr Harper while he attended the funeral and the meeting. It seemed probable to the trail boss that one would immediately follow the other. 'Where's the meeting being held?'

'The Prairie Rose.'

Virgil scooped up his hat. 'Come on,' he said to Curly. They made for the door.'

'I'm sorry about the boy,' the woman said. 'The whole town is sorry about the boy.'

Virgil turned his expressionless face to her, his grey eyes fixed on her face. 'Yes, ma'am,' he said; then he planted his hat on his head and left the eating-house. Through the window, the woman watched as the two men crossed the street, their shoulders swinging with the determination of their stride. She had told the man the town was sorry for the death of the boy but she knew that sorry didn't come close to satisfying the man's determination on vengeance.

The meeting had already begun when Virgil and Curly pushed their way into the now crowded saloon bar. A man was standing on a table at the far end of the room. He wore a black frock coat, a maroon cravat and grey trousers that sagged at the knees. He was bare-headed and his unkempt hair was almost white. He had his hands raised, imploring silence of those gathered within, but his voice was lost in the general drone of conversation.

A second man, more determined to be heard, banged a tin tray on the polished bar, producing a cymbal-like sound though devoid of any musical merit, and provoking a glare from the aproned barman, who had spent the morning making the wood of the counter gleam like pins in a gambler's cuffs.

'Quiet,' yelled Saul Patrick, for it was the newspaper-man who held the tray. 'Listen to Mr Tyrell. There's no point having a meeting if everyone's talking at the same time.' Heads were nodded, voices muttered agreement and, when Saul Patrick with extended arm motioned for the man on the table to open proceedings, silence descended.

'I'm not here to make a speech,' Mr Tyrell began. 'We all know why we're here. What I will say is that the leaders of this town and its citizens have been less diligent in upholding the law than they should have been.' Here and there an angry voice was raised, from men aggrieved by the smear of failure for, in this case, it implied cowardice, too. Once again, Tyrell raised his arms to restore order, confessing, 'I include myself in both categories. Because we don't see ourselves as fighting men we've allowed those who threaten violence to rule the town. We've turned a blind eye to events beyond the town limits so that we could pretend we had a peaceful community. We even tied the hands of our lawman, tightening his area of jurisdiction so that he had no authority to pursue criminals further than the end of Main Street. We were wrong. Perhaps peace and prosperity were the worthy aims behind our behav-iour, but we were wrong to think that they could be achieved by looking the other way.

'Two days ago, a young man, a stranger, performed a service for this town for which we were all grateful. Mr Patrick here,' he pointed at the newspaperman at his side, 'printed his exploits in *The Clarion*, but less than an hour after telling his story, that boy was dead. Shot in this very saloon. Because those who were in here that day will not testify to the contrary, his death has been recorded as fair fight.'

He paused, scanned the room, not looking to humble any of those men who could tell a different story, but hoping to see some evidence that what he was saying was having some effect.

'Tom Oates,' he continued, 'may not have been the best lawman in the West but he was *our* lawman. The man we elected to handle our troubles, to keep our homes and families safe. But that's too big a job for one man. He needed our help but it wasn't there. Clancy Jarrett murdered him out on the street just as surely as he murdered that young boy in here.'

Murmurs of agreement followed that statement. Someone in the crowd shouted out a question. 'What are we going to do about it?'

'That's what we've gathered for,' replied Tyrell, 'to decide what we do about replacing Tom Oates and what we do about Clancy Jarrett.'

Tyrell's speech had aroused a great deal of indignation but converting that to action wasn't an easy matter. The citizens of Brannigan, even when riled, were still the same storekeepers, ranch hands and business men they'd been two days ago. Although Tyrell's words had sharpened their appetite for civic responsibility, they no more relished the prospect of violence now than they had then.

The man in the crowd spoke again. 'We could organize a posse. Find Clancy Jarrett and mete out the punishment he deserves.'

'A posse wouldn't be legal,' someone answered. 'We need a sheriff to swear in deputies. Otherwise we're just a lynch mob. I'll have no part of that.'

Again, murmurs arose from those gathered in the saloon but they were silenced once more by Mr Tyrell. 'As mayor I have the authority to swear in deputies in an emergency and I'll be happy to hand out stars to any volunteers, but let it be understood that Clancy Jarrett isn't the sort of man to give up without a fight. Blood may be spilt, but whether it is or it isn't catching him is just the first part of the task. What do we do with him after that? If we lock him up we need men to guard him and there's no point bringing him to trial if no one is prepared to testify against him.'

'What the town needs,' declared Saul Patrick, 'is a new sheriff, someone with due authority to organize the arrest and trial of Clancy Jarrett, a figure of authority capable of getting the job done.'

'That's what I was coming to,' Tyrell said. 'The question is, does anyone want the job?'

Men looked at their neighbours or their boots but no one spoke up to take on the job or suggest a name for consideration.

'Can't say I'm surprised,' said Mayor Tyrell after the lapse of a few moments. 'So I propose that we send for the sheriff at Billings. We'll ask him to handle the arrest of Clancy Jarrett while we spread our net wider in search of a permanent sheriff.' The hubbub from the throng was a growing sound of agreement but the mayor wasn't finished. 'No doubt it will be necessary to assure the man from Billings that posse men will be available to him if he has need of them.' He let his gaze wander over the room and was heartened to see that many of the men gave an emphatic nod of assent.

'Mr Mayor.' A large man pushed his way forward to a point in front of Tyrell, eventually standing shoulder to shoulder with Saul Patrick. 'Mr Mayor,' he repeated, 'I am not a brave man, sir, but I am an advocate of the rule of law.'

He turned to address the room, his voice and his words flowery, like a travelling player drawing a crowd for a one-night performance. 'My name is Silas Wainwright. Although Brannigan is not my permanent place of abode I do, under the circumstances, feel compelled to give whatever assistance I am able to offer in the apprehending of the man you seek for the killing of your sheriff. Because I am ill at ease astride a horse, I cannot do this by joining a posse.'

He spread his arms, indicating the bulk of his body as proof of his words. 'However, some of you will know that I was a passenger on the coach that was subject to the attempted hold-up two days ago, an experience, I assure you, I do not wish ever to repeat.'

Wainwright's manner evoked a smattering of amusement among some of the men in the room but he ignored it and continued to speak. 'During the past two days I have heard several comments that suggest that the man who killed your sheriff was probably responsible for the attempted robbery. I cannot confirm that. Indeed, I cannot confirm that he killed the sheriff as I was not on the street at the time.

'However, I can confirm that the killing of the young man in this saloon was, in my opinion, murder. The boy made no attempt to reach for a gun nor did he involve himself in any argument with his killer. To me, as one of the trio who chased off our attackers, he was a hero who didn't deserve to die in that fashion.

'And, Mr Mayor,' he said, looking up at Tyrell who still towered over everyone in the room, 'when you apprehend the man who killed him I will testify at his trial.'

A moment of silence was broken by Mr Tyrell. 'I thank you, Mr Wainwright. I hope that when the time comes, when we have Clancy Jarrett locked in the town jail, your declaration persuades other people to come forward with what they know.'

'Amen to that,' said Saul Patrick.

'OK,' said Tyrell, 'I don't think we have anything else to discuss so I'll close the meeting and set about getting in touch with the sheriff at Billings.'

'Hold there a minute.' Virgil Jefford's rough voice rose above the general conversation as the gathering prepared to disband. Heads turned in his direction as he pushed his way through the crowd towards the table upon which the mayor stood. Curly Timms followed close behind his boss. 'We're not done here yet,' declared Virgil when he reached the front of the room, almost toe-to-toe with Silas Wainwright.

Mayor Tyrell asked the question that was on every other man's lips. 'Who are you?'

'The name is Jefford,' stated the trail boss. 'I've got a herd south of here that I'm driving to the Cheyenne railhead. That boy who was killed, his name was Walt Dickers. He was one of my boys.' His words had been listened to in silence but now there were murmurs among the crowd. 'Walt came here with two other fellows to gather provisions. I know they all arrived here because I've read the article in your newspaper and two of my horses are still in the livery at the far end of the street. The question is where are they now?'

Vainly, Virgil scanned the room again as he'd done when first entering the Prairie Rose, hoping to see Bart and Al among those gathered.

Saul Patrick answered, introducing himself to the cattleman as the proprietor of *The Clarion* and the writer of the account that had appeared in the newspaper.

'At this moment, Mr Jefford, it may not be much consolation to you to hear that the whole town is sorry about what happened to the boy, but it took his death to awaken Brannigan to the evil it harboured in allowing Clancy Jarrett to stride its streets with impunity.'

'From what I heard,' said Virgil, 'it was the death of your sheriff that did that.'

'You are right, Mr Jefford. The death of Tom Oates was the final straw, but the killing of your young rider had already kicked the conscience of the good men of this town.'

Virgil Jefford's countenance was a stone mask, that of a man unwilling to betray any belief in the newspaperman's comment. 'What about my other men? Al Dunnin and Bart Sween, what's happened to them? Where are they?'

'We don't know,' confessed Saul Patrick, who then went on to describe the events following the shooting of Sheriff Oates; how Bart, Al and Kate had been pursued from Brannigan by a gang led by Clancy Jarret. Anger showed on Virgil's face at the realization that no one had done anything to help his men and that they had been chased from the town without any interference on their behalf by the citizens.

'With the sheriff dead there was no one to organize a posse,' Saul Patrick explained, but he did so with little conviction in his words, knowing how weak they must sound to a man like Virgil Jefford.

Ascertaining that Clancy Jarrett and his men had not been seen in Brannigan since that night, the cattleman probed for information as to their current likely whereabouts. Discovering that his small farm was in the opposite direction to that in which he'd ridden out of town brought about a plethora of comments from those gathered, but it was a light, feminine voice that provided Virgil with the most useful facts.

Along with the other women of the saloon, Cherokee Lil had witnessed the meeting from the sanctuary of the area behind the long bar, but now, convinced that Virgil Jefford was determined to ride to the assistance of his missing men, she spoke up, divulging to those congregated in the Prairie Rose the facts that she knew. She told Virgil about Alice being held captive at Clancy's cabin and of Kate's intention to rescue her and ride on to Billings to seek the assistance of the law officers in that town.

'Then Jarrett's cabin is the place to begin,' declared Virgil.

Mayor Tyrell proposed the organization of a posse but Virgil wanted no part of it, he had never sought help from the law in the past; he was too old to change his ways now. He instructed Curly to find their provisions and get them back to the herd as soon as possible. Before setting out to find Bart and Al, Virgil sought out the undertaker's workshop and watched as Seth Simms unlaced the folds of the tarpaulin in which Walt Dickers's body was wrapped. After a moment of silence the undertaker asked if it was still the cattleman's intention to bury him somewhere along the cattle trail.

Virgil could guess why Bart and Al would choose to take the boy's body back to the crew for burial; a town without conscience was no place to be put in the soil. But he had listened to the mayor and the newspaperman as they'd addressed the gathering, and perhaps they'd said enough to spark a change of attitude in Brannigan's menfolk. Perhaps, too, the big man, Silas Wainwright, an outsider, had done enough to shame them into making the town a better place to live.

Also, Virgil had another, more personal matter to consider. 'No. Bury him in your cemetery. Do the best you can for him. Have your preacher say words over him. Have the citizens turn out to sing hymns. Put up a marker so that people will see his name. Walt Dickers. Age 17. Cowboy.' Virgil rummaged in his pocket and produced a handful of money which he sorted through for the undertaker's twelve dollar payment.

Virgil followed the directions he'd been given to Clancy Jarrett's cabin, his mind occupied as he rode with thoughts of young Walt and wondering how he would break the news to Charlotte, his granddaughter, when he returned home. She and Walt had grown close over those last few weeks, probably sharing an awareness of the opposite sex for the very first time. It wasn't that Virgil expected anything would come of it but he'd watched his granddaughter tease Walt in the way girls do, and he'd seen Walt strut around to the amusement of the other hands in an attempt to keep her attention.

He'd seen them together at other times, too; times when they thought themselves alone, sitting on a corral fence or watering horses at a stream, those awkward moments of young love with each of them unsure of the next word to say or move to make. When Walt had ridden off on this first trail drive he'd been wearing a new 'kerchief around his neck and it was Virgil's belief that it was a gift from Charlotte, a belief strengthened by the way Walt's fingers frequently strayed to it.

Charlotte would be distraught when he broke the news, which was why he'd chosen to have Walt buried in a proper cemetery. He doubted that she would ever visit the grave but it would settle her thoughts to know that he had been buried in a Christian churchyard and in a proper manner.

Thoughts of Charlotte and Walt still filled his mind when he reached the small cabin that had been described to him as Clancy Jarrett's abode. He approached the place carefully but even from afar and in the gathering gloom it had about it an atmosphere of being unoccupied. Dismounting in a copse about 150 yards from the shack, Virgil approached with stealth, moving from one place of concealment to another.

Eventually, standing on the porch, he pushed open the door and confirmed that there was no one inside. Anxious though he was to pursue Clancy Jarrett and find out what had happened to Bart Sween and Al Dunnin, experience told him there was little more he could do this day. He moved into the high ground above the shack and camped where he could watch over it in case the men he wanted came back. He unsaddled his horse so that it rested well during the night; in the morning there was tracking to do and a hard ride towards Billings.

CHAPTER ELEVEN

Clancy Jarrett threw the remains of his coffee into the last small flames of their morning fire, then scattered the embers with his boot, stamping where necessary to kill off any lingering life. He stood alone now on the shelf that had been their campsite for two nights, a place from which he could see the trail below and across the panorama of land that led south to the river. The sun had risen with its accustomed warmth and it had brought with it a conviction that this day Kate and the cowboys would break from cover and make their dash for Billings. He believed, he'd told Sepp, Hank and Dewey, that their quarry would, by now, think the chase was over, that having avoided capture during the storm they would expect their pursuers to return to Brannigan. So his men had ridden out that morning as they had the previous afternoon, seeking signs that would lead them to the trio and, hopefully, drive them forward to where Clancy waited to pick them off as they approached on the trail below.

The alacrity with which his plan had been adopted had

been something of a surprise to Clancy. Yesterday they had been anxious to abandon the hunt, but yesterday it had been wet and cold and no one relished exposure to such elements. Today, he assumed, rested and warm, they were ready for the challenge that lay ahead. Sepp Minto had drained his mug and thrown his saddle over his cayuse almost before Clancy had finished talking. With barely a word to the others, he'd set off into the high ground.

Dewey Shillitoe seemed hardly less anxious to be about the business, but waited for Hank Pardoe to saddle up so that they could ride out together. Clancy had watched them go, slowly picking their way down the hillside to the trail below, then setting an unhurried pace towards Brannigan. Now as he watched them, distant forms, unrecognizable if he hadn't watched their departure, they had drawn rein, were sitting side by side in conversation. One of them, Dewey Shillitoe, the taller of the two, was pointing back to where Clancy stood. Next moment, both horsemen had left the trail and were riding south towards the river, the horses galloping hard as though spurs had been roughly applied.

For an instant such seemed their urgency that Clancy thought they'd sighted Kate and the cowboys, but from his higher position he soon realized the error of that thought. From the depression that was the trail, their view was restricted. They couldn't have seen anyone south of where they'd drawn rein. From his vantage point, Clancy could see more of the land towards the river and nothing had caught his eye. The truth of the situation dawned slowly: Dewey Shillitoe and Hank Pardoe were running out on him.

A black anger gripped him and instantly he reached for his rifle. He knew they were out of range before raising it to his shoulder, but his instinct was to fire a shot after them, make it clear that he knew of their desertion and that one day he would pay them back. No one disobeyed Clancy Jarrett.

He didn't fire. Bitter though he was, he wasn't oblivious to the fact that a gunshot might be heard by Kate and her friends. Preventing them from reaching Billings, getting Jake Devane's money was, currently, more important. He wasn't going to reveal to them his position.

He kicked at the pile of ashes where the fire had been, cursing the two who had gone. He needed people around him, people who would do his bidding without question. Now, with the recent deaths of Ollie Dent and Tulsa Jones, he only had Sepp Minto upon whom he could rely. At least Sepp was loyal, he told himself, thinking how eager he'd been earlier to mount up and ride away into the high country. Suddenly, that memory wasn't a comforting thought; had he, too, been anxious to leave camp because he was deserting? Once among the hills he could ride clear in any direction. The more he considered Sepp's behaviour that morning the more certain Clancy became that Sepp would not be returning.

In a black mood Clancy saddled his horse. Perhaps Shillitoe and Pardoe were now too far away to catch, but he wasn't going to let Sepp Minto betray him. He would be travelling slowly in the hilly terrain and wouldn't be expecting pursuit. If he planned to double-cross Clancy Jarrett he wouldn't see the sun go down.

The warmth of the morning made Bart Sween impatient.

Common sense insisted that the marshal wasn't yet capable of travel but the new day had increased his desire to get Kate to Billings as soon as possible. Like Al, he was anxious to return to the cattle-drive and, once more he broached the subject of splitting trails: one of them staying with Kate and the marshal while the other struck out to join up with Virgil Jefford.

Al vetoed the idea. 'We don't know where Jarrett and his men are,' he told Bart, 'and if they're waiting for us along the trail they won't be throwing words to persuade us against going on to Billings. The marshal is much improved this morning but he ain't yet up to helping out in a fight. No, Bart, we agreed to see this through together and nothing's altered to change my mind.'

Bart had no argument against his friend's words so, resigned to the fact that they wouldn't be moving on for another day, he collected his rifle and announced that he would scout around in case Clancy and his men were still in the vicinity.

Bart returned to the cave an hour later. Kate was helping Hec Masters to drink water from a canteen. She stood when he entered and crossed to where Al was tending the horses so that she could listen to Bart's report.

'I saw two men riding south towards the river. They could have been two of our pursuers but they were a bit too far distant to be positive. If the marshal had been better fixed it might have been an opportunity to strike out for Billings. If they've divided their force we'll stand a better chance of getting through.'

Al said nothing. Eager as he was for an end to the situation in which they were involved it seemed to him they'd be acting on guesswork if they moved out now because of the sighting of two distant riders.

Kate said she needed to leave the cave for a while, needed a few minutes of privacy. She indicated a pile of clean undergarments she'd taken from her bag. Neither cowboy was in favour of her going out alone but nor did they know how to argue against it. Bart told her to stay among the surrounding trees and suggested a spot where he'd seen a fall of rainwater where she could wash.

Gathering her belongings, Kate left the cave. A few steps beyond the entrance she paused to make sure that neither man followed her. The reason for her hesitation had nothing to do with modesty or distrust of the men's intentions. Concealed among her clean garments were bundles of paper money. During the night she'd reached the decision that she and Alice deserved some of the money.

Perhaps the cowboys wouldn't be interested in Clancy's claim that the money was his but Marshal Masters certainly was. Weak as he was, she'd still seen the wheels of his mind working, pondering the relationship between Jake and Clancy and reaching the conclusion that the money was stolen.

Although yesterday it would have been hard for her to believe such a thing of Jake Devane, today was different. Perhaps some of it was the proceeds of stagecoach robberies but, equally, some of it must have been the result of his gambling exploits. No one knew how much had been in the bag so she'd left several wads in the bottom, but had brought the rest with her to squirrel away until she and Alice were reunited. They would retrieve it when Marshal Masters was long gone from the territory.

*

Sepp Minto rubbed his sleeve over his mouth as he watched Kate move further up the slope. He had almost missed her, her route uphill following a different path from that which he'd anticipated the cowboys would use, following his sighting of them yesterday. When he became aware of her she was only five steps away from the boulder behind which he had stationed himself. This gave him only enough time to press himself against the rock so that she didn't see him as she passed by.

He watched her for a moment, relishing the thoughts that filled his head, unable to suppress the smirk that almost bubbled over into a laugh of anticipation. Perhaps Sepp would have been more cautious if Clancy hadn't dragged him away from that Mexican girl in the Red Garter, but it had been almost two weeks since his last visit to town and female company had become a predominant need.

He let her move ahead, almost a dozen paces, casting around for any sign that might indicate that she was not alone, but none were evident.

Kate sensed Sepp's presence when he was three steps behind. By the time a cry of alarm had formed in her throat a large, grimy hand had clamped her mouth closed and the burly weight of her attacker was lifting her from her feet, forcing her to the ground. She struggled, tried vainly to bite the fingers that were held against her face and twisted her head to and fro in an attempt to loosen Sepp's grip.

He was grinning; his teeth, clenched together, showed behind slightly parted lips. He was enjoying her struggles, knowing that she hadn't the strength to compete with him. 'If you scream when I take away my hand,' he snarled, 'I'll knock your head off your shoulders. Do you understand?'

Kate continued to twist and struggle, and swung the bundle she carried at Sepp's head. It had no harmful effect, of course, but when bundles of money tumbled from within the folds it brought an appreciative laugh from her assailant. With his free hand he wrenched it from her grip and shook it until the contents were scattered on the ground.

'Just what I was looking for,' he declared, then moved swiftly and violently. Releasing his grip over her mouth he slapped her across both cheeks. The blows were delivered with stunning force and for a moment it seemed that he had knocked the girl senseless. Grabbing the bodice of her blouse he pulled her head clear of the ground.

She opened her eyes, slowly, as though recovering her senses, but it was all an act. The blows had hurt but hadn't done anything to damage her instinct for survival. She hoped that by adopting the tactic of appearing weaker than she really was would get him to relax his hold on her. She screamed, knowing that his reaction would be to hit her again, but while he did that he failed to notice her right hand scrabbling across the ground to find a rock. The rock was hard and rough.

Sepp Minto was preparing to hit her again when her right arm swung in an arc. The jagged edge of the rock she held smashed against his cheekbone with all the force she could muster. She drew it down his face, splitting the skin in a three-inch gash from which blood splattered down on to her dress. Sepp yelled and raised a hand to the cut. Kate struck again, this time hitting the corner of his eye. He fell away from her. She pushed him away, tried to scramble to her feet but freedom wasn't so easily gained.

Sepp Minto had a history of bar-room brawls and hadn't lost many. His left arm snaked out and his hand fastened around Kate's ankle. Slowly he pulled her back towards him. He was grunting, calling her names and uttering threats that he would surely carry out when she was completely in his power. She kicked backwards, her booted foot crashing against his nose. She kicked again: the second time producing a crack and a squelch that implied she'd broken it. Sepp yelled and released his hold on the girl's leg.

She got to her feet and began running back down the hillside but Sepp, propelled by fury, followed instantly, his huge strides rapidly closing the gap. Kate knew she wouldn't win a race. She stopped and calmly turned to meet him. As he approached she produced Jake's derringer which she'd put in the pocket of her skirt back at Clancy's cabin. She waited for him to come closer, her eyes fixed on his, sending a message that she would die before she let him touch her again.

At the sight of the small gun, Sepp stopped. The way she held it told him she was prepared to use it, and she did. Pulling the trigger was a steady, deliberate act. The resulting click surprised both of them. Once again she tried to fire the weapon but the result was the same. The gun was empty. Sepp's grin was born of relief but spread into a leer of total triumph. From behind his back he produced a huge hunting knife.

'When I'm finished with you I'm going to slice you into tiny strips,' he told her.

Sepp took a step forward and Kate took the only course

of action that was left to her. She threw the derringer at him. Sepp anticipated the manoeuvre and flicked it aside with his own weapon.

'Now you're mine,' he said, and was upon her in an instant. Kate tried to fight him off, began kicking, spitting and biting as she struggled against the big man, but he forced her backwards until she was up against the rock face of the hillside.

That was how Al came across them. Kate's first scream had brought him uphill at a run. His first instinct had been to use his rifle but there was was an equal chance of hitting Kate as there was of felling her attacker. Unaware of the hunting knife that Sepp still held in his hand, Al gripped him by the shoulder and pulled him away from the girl.

Although surprised by Al's arrival, Sepp retaliated as he would in a bar-room free for all. He swung at Al, the knife scything the air, forcing the cowboy to stumble away. Kate attempted to hold on to Sepp's arm but he was too strong for her and cast her away from him with such force that she was unable to remain on her feet.

Al gripped his rifle with both hands, yelled for Sepp to surrender, but the man's response was of a completely different nature. As Kate had done earlier with the derringer, he flung his knife at his adversary. The huge blade embedded itself into the cowboy's right shoulder. Involuntarily, Al pulled the trigger of his rifle but the shot flew harmlessly into the air as he stumbled backwards and fell to the ground.

Certain that his opponent was at his mercy, Sepp drew his revolver and began to advance. Behind him, Kate picked up another lump of rock and threw it at Sepp's head. The blow was nothing more than a distraction, but that was all Al needed. Despite the pain in his shoulder he realigned his rifle and fired. Sepp jerked back, his eyes widened, then his legs buckled under him. Al fired again to make sure the fight was finished.

With Sepp dead, Kate turned her attention to Al. The knife was high in the shoulder which meant it was unlikely to be life threatening, but his pallor and the lines of strain etched across his brow were a sure indication of the cowboy's pain. She helped him to his feet in an urgent desire to get him back to the cave. They both knew there could be other men in the vicinity.

In response to the rifle shots, Bart had begun to make his way cautiously up the hillside. Relieving Kate of Al's weight, he helped his friend back to the cave. Kate recounted the event and Al confirmed that he recognized the man as one of their pursuers.

'Sepp Minto,' Kate stated. 'Which means that Clancy won't be far away.'

'That body needs to be hidden,' Bart declared. 'If Clancy Jarrett finds it he might be able to follow our trail back here.'

Al tried to rise, uttering words that amounted to the fact that he would accompany his friend, but both Bart and Kate forbade it. Bart told him he had to remain in the cave. 'If I don't come back it'll be up to you to protect these people from Jarrett.'

Kate thought about the money strewn on the ground near the body. Bart, she realized, was bound to see it and for a moment she wondered what his reaction would be. But that moment passed. Al's wound needed her attention. If he wasn't fit enough to raise his rifle then the probability was that Clancy would win and the money wouldn't be the only thing she'd lose.

Bart was aware that his parting words had been less than encouraging; instead of promoting the idea that now there was only Clancy Jarrett standing between themselves and a clear road to Billings, he had left them pondering on the closeness of death. Pessimism wasn't his usual brand, and he had intended his words as an excuse for his wounded friend to stay in the cave, but he knew that he'd cast doubt over their ability to survive this situation. He hadn't travelled more than a hundred yards before his prophecy of doom came close to fulfilment.

A shot rang out which carried Bart's hat from his head. He dived for cover, seeking the protection of a fallen tree. Another shot gouged out a huge splinter from the old bark, which flew away, yards beyond where Bart lay. He knew by the sound of the report and the power of the bullet hitting timber that the gunman had a rifle. He was outgunned. Not wanting to be encumbered with a rifle if he had to move the body any distance, he had left the cave armed only with his revolver. Going on sound alone, he knew his opponent was out of pistol range.

'I could have taken your head off with the first shot,' a voice called, 'but I'm a reasonable man. It's Kate and the money I want. Give them to me and you and your partner can go.'

Bart looked around. Lying on the ground didn't allow for much of a view and with little leeway for raising his head to see more of the surrounding terrain, any move he made was going to involve a massive slice of chance. Behind him, a scattering of shrubbery promised alternative cover and from there perhaps he'd find an opportunity to dodge uphill. Drawing Clancy Jarrett away from those in the cave had to be his objective, but Clancy already knew he'd come from further down the slope, so even if the gunman followed him up the hillside it would only be a temporary halt to his pursuit of Kate.

Bart rued the fact that he hadn't told his friends to saddle up and ride out for Billings if they heard gunfire. Hec Masters would just have to take his chances along with everyone else. But Bart didn't let his mind dwell on situations that weren't possible. He had to do something about his current predicament or else Clancy Jarrett would kill him where he now lay.

Clancy was calling to him again, repeating his offer, a tone in his voice that implied his belief in his total domination of the situation. Bart removed his hat, scuttled to one end of the tree trunk and ventured a look in the direction of the voice. It was his first real sight of Clancy Jarrett, a long, slender man who, like himself, had several days' growth of hair on his face. He was a dark-haired man, unremarkable except for the Winchester which he held loosely in both hands. The ease with which he held it informed Bart that he was accustomed to using a gun, that his marksmanship was probably a skill on which he prided himself. Bart knew that any move that exposed him for more than an instant was likely to be his last.

'Did you kill Sepp? I found his body up there,' Clancy called. 'He was a tough man. Must have been some fight. Wish I'd seen it.'

While Clancy spoke, Bart made his move, edging back a little before raising himself to his knees, then launching himself forward in a diving, rolling motion that carried him into the bushes behind. Bullets zipped and pinged around him, twigs spun through the air. He felt an impact on his left foot but no pain. The high heel of his left riding boot flew into the air, then went skittering downhill.

There was a natural trench behind the bush into which Bart dropped, breathing heavily, aware that good fortune had smiled on him and saved him from harm. The trench was no more than six yards long, becoming shallow at one end, reducing its effective protection to about half that length. Still, he took what advantage he could, crawling away as far as possible from his original landing place. He drew his pistol and risked a look over the lip of the trench.

Clancy Jarrett wasn't where Bart had last seen him. Indeed, at first he couldn't see any sign of his hunter, prompting him to raise his head higher. There were several places that would provide adequate cover for the rifleman but Bart couldn't see any telltale sign to pinpoint his whereabouts. His inspection took in rocks and a scattering of trees and bushes, giving most attention to those behind which Clancy could hide upright. Of necessity, he couldn't allow his attention to settle on any place, his eyes sweeping the terrain, seeking the likely location of the next attack, but it was sound not sight that alerted him to the boulder which was Clancy's cover. They were separated by thirty feet, and the unmistakable ratchet sound of a rifle's lever carried clearly across the space between.

Clancy stepped from behind the boulder and fired twice, the closeness of the bullets convincing Bart that they hadn't been wild shots, that Clancy knew his exact location. At least now, he told himself, his foe was within pistol range, but as a gunman he knew he was no match for Clancy. However, Clancy's next burst of firing was answered by Bart. Two shots struck the boulder close to Clancy's head, their ricochets removing chips of stone and forcing him to seek refuge. Heartened by Clancy's withdrawal, Bart fired twice more, keeping his adversary pinned down while he made a dash for a new position.

With only two bullets left, Bart knew he had little hope of survival. His only motive for moving was a desire to protect those in the cave, although even that, he admitted to himself, was little more than a pipe dream. Even so, as he fired the shots that kept Clancy Jarrett behind the boulder, he got to his feet and began to run towards a clump of trees higher up the slope, which would be his next refuge.

He was only two strides into his sprint when he stumbled. He'd forgotten about the damage to his left boot. Unbalanced by the missing heel, he fell. A bullet flew overhead, then another struck the ground where a moment before he had been. Now he was slithering downhill with increasing momentum. Another shot followed him but didn't hit. He travelled thirty feet, tumbling over and over, dirt and scree spreading in his wake. There was a moment when he thought the fall might carry him beyond the reach of his enemy but that hope ended when he came up against a formidable rock which halted his progress and drove the wind from his body. More important, he also lost his grip on his revolver and he watched it slide further down the hillside.

Clancy Jarrett stood on the slope with his rifle in his hands. He didn't rush forward to finish off the cowboy who had thwarted the hold-up before attempting to assist Kate's flight to Billings. In this moment of triumph he afforded himself a self-congratulatory grin. That grin remained on his face until he stood over Bart, gloating at the fact that he had the first of those he had chased for more than two days at his mercy.

'Got to tell you,' he said, 'I lied earlier when I said I was a reasonable man.' He shifted the rifle in his hands, bringing the barrel round to point at Bart's head.

Another voice broke the stillness on the hillside, a firm voice that suggested its owner was a man accustomed to command.

'Are you Clancy Jarrett?'

Clancy turned, instantly curious as to how a man on a horse had come so close without advertising his presence. He was an older man with a dark, weather-beaten face that was lined by the cares of life's struggles. Across his knees lay an unsheathed Winchester. He was almost motionless, casual in the way he sat his horse and asked his question, as though he'd stopped a schoolyard dust-up rather than a fight for survival. Clancy didn't answer, merely turned his head as though confused by the interruption. The man spoke again.

'My name's Virgil Jefford,' he said. 'You killed one of my boys. You're not killing another.' With the final word and without adjusting the position of the rifle by even an inch, he pulled the trigger to send Clancy Jarrett on his way to hell. Then he fired again to make sure he got there.

An hour later the group from the cave were ready to leave. No one else had come into their vicinity so they deduced that the departing riders seen by Bart earlier in the day had indeed been the remaining gang members. It was unlikely they would meet up again.

Virgil Jefford assumed leadership of the group. He had been a figure of authority for thirty years, the mantle sat easily on his shoulders. He declared Hec Masters to be in no condition to ride far or alone and set aside the marshal's desire to head back to Billings. Virgil's cattle were more important than acting as nursemaid to the wounded lawman and he, Bart and Al were all needed to drive the herd on to Wyoming.

Kate, too, had hoped to journey on to Billings where she could be reunited with her sister. She had volunteered to be Hec's companion on the trip, but Virgil vetoed that idea. If Hec suffered a relapse, he stated, the girl wasn't physically strong enough to cope with him. Although he would rather head due south, Virgil declared that the only sensible solution was for him and his men to escort the girl and the wounded lawman to the closer township of Brannigan. It meant another delay in their return to the herd but one which he deemed necessary.

Hec Masters queried the need of taking with them the bodies of Clancy Jarrett and Sepp Minto.

'If the citizens of Brannigan want to see them they can come and get them,' Virgil stated in his typical bluff manner. 'Otherwise, the wild beasts of the mountain can feast on them. They're dead and gone to me. I won't think of them again.'

Virgil's cold assessment came as no surprise to Bart and Al. He had been single-minded all his life, only interested in the advancement of his own business. It was the way of the West, holding tightly to your own beliefs and possessions.

Al, too, had his roots in the West. When, finally and reluctantly, everyone admitted to the sense of Virgil's plan, he took Kate aside.

'I believe you left some of your belongings on the hillside,' he said. 'Perhaps we should go and collect them.' He gave her a wink that was unobserved by anyone else, letting her know that he'd seen the money. Kate thought he wanted her to hand the money over to Marshal Masters, but that wasn't the case. In these parts, where true law officers were sometimes a week away, a fuzzy line existed between justice and the law. Al was no stranger to it. He didn't consider himself a criminal, just a survivor, someone who had sometimes found it necessary to live by his own interpretation of right and wrong. He listened to Kate's explanation for being in possession of Jake Devane's money as they climbed the hillside, and grinned when she admitted that she'd left some of the money in the bag to hand over to the marshal.

'There might be a reward for the return of that portion,' he said laughing, 'but just to be on the safe side I'll help you hide the rest of it. You and your sister can come back for it when the marshal's gone back to Billings.' He didn't know what plans she had for the money, didn't even want to know, but perhaps Kate and Alice could start afresh. He hadn't known Jake Devane, but he would have been surprised if the gambler had wanted the girls to be anything other than his whores in Cheyenne, but perhaps they believed something different. If they did they might get some benefit from the money.

They heard Virgil Jefford calling for them further down the mountain.

'Time to go,' said Al, rolling a heavy stone into the crevice which now housed the money. 'Time to go.'